C0-DKP-768

If It's Not One Thing—
It's Another!

"Well, what's wrong with your mom and Sam?" Harry asked, raking up a big pile of leaves. "Do you think they're going to get a divorce?"

"Of course not! They're just fighting about soccer—it's no big deal."

"I don't know, Cynthia," Harry said, taking off his glasses and waving them around. "That's sometimes just how these things start."

"Thanks a lot, Harry," I said disgustedly. "Thanks just a whole big bunch," and I stomped off down the street.

What a creep! I didn't want him to see how upset I was. But what if Harry was right? What if Mom and Sam were going to get a divorce? I hated it when Daddy left, and now to think Sam could leave too . . .

Jean Davies Okimoto

It's Just Too Much

AN ARCHWAY PAPERBACK
Published by POCKET BOOKS • NEW YORK

An Archway Paperback published by
POCKET BOOKS, a Simon & Schuster division of
GULF & WESTERN CORPORATION
1230 Avenue of the Americas, New York, N.Y. 10020

Copyright © 1980 by Jean Davies Okimoto

Published by arrangement with G. P. Putnam's Sons
Library of Congress Catalog Card Number: 80-15411

All rights reserved, including the right to reproduce
this book or portions thereof in any form whatsoever.
For information address G. P. Putnam's Sons,
200 Madison Avenue, New York, N.Y. 10016

ISBN: 0-671-43492-6

First Archway Paperback printing March, 1982

10 9 8 7 6 5 4 3 2 1

AN ARCHWAY PAPERBACK and colophon are
trademarks of Simon & Schuster.

Printed in the U.S.A.

IL 7+

*Always and forever, to Joe, Steve, Dylan,
Katie, the gentle cat, Amy, the fire horse,
and
for Charles Mercer*

It's Just Too Much

One

Right now things are not so great in my life. My best friend, Trae, is turning beautiful. It is not easy to have a best friend who is turning beautiful when you are not. In fact, I would say that she is the first most beautiful girl in our entire sixth grade class, and possibly the entire school.

It was especially bothering me today. It was Friday, and Trae and I had walked home from school together and were doing cartwheels and stuff on our front lawn. It was a beautiful spring, Seattle day. The sky was very blue and the grass was bright green. The rhododendrons from our neighbor's yard had big blossoms all over the place, and the day smelled like the perfume I gave Mom for her birthday last year.

Harry Zimmerman came zooming by us on

his ten-speed bike. He was riding no-handed and waving his arms around, then all of a sudden Harry went flying through the air and landed, sprawled right in front of us, on the lawn. His glasses fell off and his bike had crashed down on top of him. Harry, who I still call Harry Z for zero, is not my favorite person on our block or in my class, or in the whole world for that matter. But I still was afraid he might be hurt.

"Harry! Are you okay?"

Harry jumped right up and put his glasses back on. "How did you like my stunt?"

"Your stunt?"

"Sure. I'm practicing to be a Hollywood stunt man. And then after that I'll be a big movie producer," he said, turning to Trae. "I'll make you a star!" Then Harry got back on his ten-speed bike and rode off, but he rode around the rock that was in the street.

"Harry is so dumb," I said to Trae while I did a back bend.

"Sometimes I think he's cute," she said, sliding her feet on the grass. Trae keeps trying to do the splits, but she can't get all the way down like I can.

"He's almost a midget and he thinks he is an expert on everything. I have lived on the same block with Harry Z my whole life and I know all about him. Stunt! Ha! Harry just fell off his bike and his stupid bike even still has those training wheels on it.''

"Well, those training wheels do look pretty silly," she admitted.

"They are ridiculous. And then trying to pretend he planned it and saying all that stuff about 'I'll make you a star.' Harry Z can't even fall off a bike like a normal person."

"I thought it was sort of funny," Trae said, smiling.

I didn't say anything. I suppose she thought it was funny because she was the one he said he'd make a star. Not that I wanted Harry to say stuff like that to me or anything like that, but I was getting sick of everyone noticing her all the time. Trae Kaplan has green eyes that are huge, kind of like a cat's eyes, and thick blond hair that never gets stringy. She also has lots of perfectly white straight teeth. Even Larry is paying attention to her. And things are confusing enough about me and Larry without having my best friend turn beautiful.

Larry is going to be my stepbrother soon. His father, Sam, is getting married to my mother. Our parents are both divorced. My little sister, Sara, and I love Sam a lot, and we think this marriage is a good idea. At least the part about Sam is a good idea. But I'm not so sure about the stepbrother part. I really wonder what that's going to be like.

Sara doesn't worry about it. She's seven and

is almost finished with the first grade. Sara is expecting the tooth fairy any day now because some of her teeth are falling out. But the only thing Sara ever seems to worry about is stuff like coloring in the lines. And David, who is eight, who is also going to be our stepbrother, likes to color in the lines too. When I was their age, I was the type that didn't color in the lines. In fact, I thought coloring books were boring. I liked to make up my own stuff to color—especially I would cut out my name in giant letters . . . Cynthia Ann Browne . . . and make all the letters striped and polka-dotted. But now I don't know what type I am, except that I am not the type that anyone would want to make a star. In our class, we have fourteen girls. There are the bra people and the no-bra people. I am one of the five no-bra people. Trae is one of the nine bra people, and I'm sure Larry has especially noticed that.

Larry is in the sixth grade too, only he goes to a different school. He and David live with their mother. We all live in Seattle, but Larry and David live in the North End and we live in the Mount Baker neighborhood, which is more in the South End.

Sometimes I think the whole world is getting divorced. I don't think I will ever get married because all that happens is that you just end up getting divorced. Harry's mother, Mrs. Zimmerman, is divorced. My mom and dad are divorced. Larry and David's mother and Sam are divorced. Trae's mother and father got a divorce, and now her mother is married to a man named Stan. My great Aunt Gertrude says the next thing you know, Santa and Mrs. Claus will be getting a divorce and the elves will visit Santa on weekends. When great Aunt Gertrude said that, it really upset Sara because she still believes. I will never get married, unless, of course, to someone like Richie Hinkley who is the cutest boy in our class.

Trae stopped trying to do the splits and started doing sit-ups. Her mother told her that would be good for her figure. My mom only tells me not to bite my fingernails.

"Mom's taking me to the zoo tomorrow," Trae said. "We're going to see the new male gorilla they got to be Mabel's mate."

"Will you be at that big thing station KWJR is having at the zoo about Mabel's new husband?"

"Sure, that's why we're going. KWJR is going to play romantic music to the gorillas and the wedding march and the first one hundred kids get some rice to throw up in the air. They're also giving out T-shirts that say 'KWJR MABEL'S WEDDING.' I wish you'd come too."

"I'd love to go—but I can't. Larry and David are coming tomorrow and Mom and Sam are taking us to Schwartzes' summer place on

Whidbey Island. I think my dad and his girl friend, Ellen, said something about taking Sara and me to see the new gorilla. But I'd rather go to the KWJR wedding to see it."

"Yeah—a gorilla wedding would be great. When are your mom and Sam getting married?"

"Exactly three weeks from tomorrow. I'm really excited!"

"Do you get to be in it?"

"Oh sure." I had my mother's wedding all figured out. There I would be in this gorgeous pink dress with lace and satin and velvet and ribbons on it, and I would have a body permanent, walking down the aisle in front of my mother, carrying a huge basket of rose petals— throwing them to the left and right, scattering them over the heads of the hundreds of people at the wedding. It would be fantastic. I didn't have a doubt that the wedding would be exactly like that.

Trae had to go home. As I watched her walk down the street, I saw Harry come zooming out of his driveway, following her on his bike and making stupid faces at her and waving his arms around. Harry thinks that is romantic. Harry is a jerk.

Two

Mom told me to walk down to Harry's and ask him if he'd feed our animals while we were at Whidbey for the weekend. I didn't especially want to, but Mom thinks Harry is the most reliable person on the block when there is money involved. She told me to tell Harry that she would pay him a dollar.

We have quite a few animals and they are all mine. There's Martha, my cat, Mildred, my canary, Ernie and Burt, my two hamsters, some fish that I didn't name, and Howard, my guinea pig. I don't like the idea of trusting my animals to a person like Harry Zimmerman. Besides that, we have to give him a key to the house so he can get in to feed them—and he'll have to come in my room. That's where my animals live, and I can't stand the thought of

Harry Z being in my room. It might get contaminated.

I walked down to Harry's house and saw Mrs. Zimmerman sitting in the bushes on top of a bag of fertilizer, drinking beer. That's how Mrs. Zimmerman always does the gardening. I asked Harry about it once and he said that she hates gardening and that her favorite springtime activity is drinking beer. Harry said she worries about what the neighbors think of their yard looking so bad, but she discovered the neighbors don't mind so much if they think she's trying.

So she bought these gardening tools and sits in the bushes on a bag of fertilizer, and when neighbors walk by she waves to them and digs a little in the dirt. She doesn't know the names of any flowers. Harry told me that if the neighbors talk about gardening, she just sticks to basic words like "flower" and "dirt."

Our yard is tied for first place with the Zimmermans' for the worst yard on the block. But Mom says it has an advantage because in the summer you can tell people who are trying to find your house that it's the one on the left side of the street with no flowers and a brown lawn. My mother gave up gardening about the same time she gave up making beds and ironing—it's been about four years now, I think.

Mrs. Zimmerman waved to me from the bushes and took a sip of her beer. She sure looked comfortable on that bag of fertilizer. I wonder if maybe she stuffed it with a pillow. "Hi, Cynthia," she said. "Harry's in the kitchen—just go on in."

"Thanks," I said. "Sure is a nice day."

"Beautiful—I love doing yard work on a day like this," she said, wiggling a weed next to the fertilizer bag.

I went inside and found Harry in the kitchen making pancakes. Harry thinks he is a gourmet cook and has this thing about prunes. He puts prunes in everything. This morning he was making prune pancakes.

"Hi, Cynthia," he said, throwing prunes in the pancake batter. "Wanna have some pancakes?"

"I'm not crazy about prunes in pancakes, Harry. I can't stay long anyway. I just came down because Mom asked me to ask you if you would feed our animals. We're going to Whidbey this weekend. She said she'd pay a dollar."

Harry stopped stirring the pancake batter. He went over to the sink and washed his hands. "Exactly how many animals are involved in this job?" he asked.

"Harry, you know—Martha, Mildred, Ernie and—"

"Just a minute, I'll have to get my book." Harry went up to his room and came back with a little black book. He had a pencil stuck behind his ear that kept falling off. Harry leafed

9

through his little black book and kept trying to get the pencil to stay stuck behind his ear. Then he wet his lips and touched the end of the pencil to the tip of his tongue.

"Names, please," he said.

"Names? What d'ya mean, names?"

"Names of the animals involved here. I need to know the names, type of animal, and some other information."

"Harry, this is ridiculous—you know very well—"

"Names, please," Harry said again, licking the end of the pencil.

"Oh all right," I said disgustedly. "Martha, Mildred—"

"Just a minute," he said, writing down "Martha" in his little black book. "Type of animal?"

"Harry, you know very well Martha is a cat!"

"Umm-hmm, all right, Martha—cat," he said, writing down "cat" next to Martha's name in his dumb book. "Next?"

"Mildred. Harry, this is going to take all day. Do you want the dollar or don't you?"

"Type of animal?" he said, ignoring me.

"CANARY!" I shouted, "MILDRED IS A CANARY!"

"Don't shout, please. Next?"

"Ernie and Burt—my hamsters. You gave them to me in the fourth grade, Harry, when you found out you were allergic. I don't believe this! I absolutely don't believe this!"

"One at a time, please," Harry said, writing down "Ernie" in his stupid book.

"Type of animal?"

"HAMSTER! YOU IDIOT—HAMSTER!"

"Cynthia," Harry said, taking off his glasses and talking in this voice as if he were talking to someone in the first grade, "I need this information if I am going to do this job properly. Would you like to eat some prune pancakes while I'm getting the information?"

"No," I said, trying with all my might to keep from dumping the prune pancake batter on top of Harry's head. "I do not want prune pancakes."

"All right, all right—there's no charge for the pancakes," Harry said, putting his glasses back on. "Next animal, please." At this point I decided that I didn't have much choice but to go along with him and his dumb book. And Harry Z actually went on with this for all the rest of the animals. He listed my fish separately, and he even wanted me to describe each fish. He said he needed that information since my fish don't have names. I really couldn't believe it. Finally Harry took off his glasses and stuck the pencil behind his ear only it fell out again. "The charges are as follows: one cat named Martha— fifty cents, one canary named Mildred—fifteen cents, two hamsters named Ernie and Burt—

twenty cents each, nameless fish—one cent each, total ten cents, and one guinea pig named Howard—thirty-five cents. The total bill will come to one dollar and fifty cents."

"That's a rip-off, Harry! Mom said she'd pay a dollar. You've always done it for a dollar! You're just doing this because you know Helene will be gone too, and we don't have anyone else on the block to ask." I was really mad. It was bad enough to have to sit there while Harry wrote down all that junk in his dumb book, but now to get ripped off too was just too much.

"That's it. One dollar and fifty cents. Take it or leave it," Harry said with this smug look as he shut his book.

"Oh, I'll call Mom." I was hoping she would think of a way to get out of this. I went over to the phone that was on the kitchen wall and dialed our number.

"Hi Mom . . . it's me."

"Cynthia, what's taking you so long? Sam's here and we're almost ready to go."

"Oh, Harry got this dumb book and—oh never mind—Harry says it'll cost a dollar fifty to feed the animals."

Mom laughed. "Well, since Harry has a monopoly tell him that's okay."

I was so disgusted. I don't know why Mom laughed anyway. Harry is not funny. "Okay, I'll be right home." I hung up the phone.

"She said 'okay' Harry, but I think it's a big

rip-off . . . And DON'T touch anything in my room!''

"I am a thoroughly reliable animal feeder, Cynthia.''

"You are a thoroughly reliable rip-off, Harry Z. Good-bye,'' I said, walking out and slamming the door.

Harry stuck his head out the door and yelled after me, "Don't you want some prune pancakes?''

"NO,'' I yelled back. "I DO NOT WANT PRUNE PANCAKES BECAUSE I DO NOT WANT TO THROW UP!''

As I walked home I thought about trying to rig up an automatic animal feeding system so we would never ever have to ask Harry Z again. I'm not good at rigging up stuff though, so I decided that one thing I would do would be to put Vaseline on the doorknob to my room right before we would leave for the weekend. I just refuse to let Harry get away with this.

Three

When I got home from Harry's, Mom said we had to leave right away so we wouldn't miss the ferry to Whidbey. I went up to my room to get my sleeping bag and was looking in the bathroom for the Vaseline when she yelled up to me to get going. I never did find the Vaseline to put on my doorknob, which meant I would have to think of something else to do to Harry.

It made me mad that Mom was bugging me to hurry up because when I came in the house Larry and David were getting a bunch of stuff out of the refrigerator to eat. It's not even their house, but they always come in and go right to the refrigerator, taking stuff without even asking, and acting like they own the place. Not even Harry does that.

One of my favorite things to eat is Ding-

Dongs. Since Larry and David have been coming over on the weekends all the time, I've been hiding the Ding-Dongs in my room. I put them in this box in my closet and I wrote "Old Underwear for Goodwill" on the box.

When Mom decided to get married to Sam I was worried at first if it would be okay for me to love my real father and Sam too. Mom told me then that love isn't like a Ding-Dong, so if you give it away to one person, there's none left for anyone else and you have to choose who to give it to. She said love is something you can give to lots of people and there's always more. It's a good thing love isn't like Ding-Dongs. Because, with Larry and David around, if it was I would get none.

When we got in the car, Larry and David had a bunch of food with them. Larry had a bag of Doritos and he had eaten almost half of it, and David was eating a banana. We had just gotten that bag of Doritos when Mom went to the store yesterday, and here it was half eaten up already. There probably weren't any bananas left either, and David was just sitting there stuffing it in his face. I thought he looked like a little monkey.

"Gimme some of those," I said to Larry, grabbing the Dorito bag. I looked in the bag. Now there were only a few crumbs left. "They're almost gone!"

"Well, you could've had 'em whenever you wanted. We never get Doritos at our house."

"So that doesn't mean you have to eat up all ours," I said. Mom turned around from the front seat.

"The food is for everyone around here. Listen, when we're on the ferry we'll get you all a hot dog."

"Look—there's a wabbit just like ours!" Sara said, pointing to a car in the next lane that looked like our car.

"Wabbit! Ha-ha-ha wabbit . . . wook at the wittle wabbit!" Larry said, making fun of Sara.

I gave Larry a dirty look. I felt like yelling at him, but Mom gets so upset if we start to fight at all. She's used to it if Sara and I get into fights, but with Larry and David it's not like that. She acts very strange. For example, I absolutely know that if I had made fun of Sara saying "wabbit," Mom would have said to me that it doesn't take any talent to make fun of another person and for me to knock it off. But she didn't say that to Larry, and Sam didn't say anything either.

Mostly what Mom and Sam have been doing is taking us to the movies a lot, and also to 31 Flavors, and now today taking us all up to Whidbey for the weekend.

Mom also gave me this big lecture about Larry and David right after she and Sam de-

16

cided to get married. She said that Larry and David would have to get used to Sam living with me and Sara. Mom said it might be hard for them to only see Sam on weekends, while Sara and I will get to live with him all the time. She said I should be very understanding about this and try to be very nice to them. She also said we would all be doing a lot of fun things on the weekends together—at least on the weekends when Sara and I weren't visiting our father—and she was sure we would all have a good time.

Well, I am not so sure about this at all. And I am especially not interested in being understanding when the Doritos get all eaten up by them.

David was still stuffing the banana in his mouth and Sara was sitting there saying ''wabbit'' over and over again, kind of to herself, trying to say it right. The VW Rabbit that we just got is new. My mom used to have this old Ford that finally broke down and died recently. Mom sold it to the gas station man for two hundred dollars, which I don't think is very much money for a car. Then she and Sam bought the Rabbit together, and it's supposed to be our new family car. It's bright yellow and has a sunroof; you just turn this little handle and the sunroof opens up. Sam always lets me uncrank the sunroof on nice days during the week. But on the weekends he lets Larry or David do it.

I miss my mom's old car. The Rabbit is a nice color, but it's too new. It also has a litter basket in the front seat. Sam said we should all not mess up the new car and should put the litter in the litter basket. My mom's old car was a litter basket—the whole car. Mom doesn't care about cars much and it was a big mess. My father, who is a very clean person, used to yell at her a lot about all of that. I am hoping that Sam doesn't turn into too much of a very clean person.

We got to the ferry line and Sam bought the ticket. He had to pay for the car and for four passengers, even though there were six people in the car. That's because on the ferry you don't have to pay if you are under twelve, and David and Sara go free. We all got out of the car and went up the stairs from the lower deck to the upper deck. The lower deck is the car part of the boat and the upper deck is the people part. Sara and David ran on ahead and got in line for food.

The way you get the food on the ferry is sort of like the lunch line at school. Larry and I and Mom and Sam got in line behind David and Sara. When we got up to the man who was taking the orders, the man said to David, "What a pretty little girl you are—and what would you like?"

David said, "I'm a boy and I'd like a hot dog." Then the man looked at Sara and said, "What would you like, young man?"

Sara said, "I'm a girl and I'd like a hot dog." Larry and I cracked up, and Mom and Sam were laughing too. We got our hot dogs and also french fries and Cokes and carried our trays to a table by the window.

I finished my french fries before everyone else, and Larry let me have some of his. "Here, young man," he said, and we all laughed.

By the time the boat got to the Whidbey ferry landing, Sara and David said "young man" and "what a pretty little girl" to each other about eighty-six times and it was getting to be not so funny.

Whidbey Island is beautiful. It has big evergreen trees and some farms. Lots of people have summer places there, and some people live there all year round too. There are evergreen trees all over the place around Seattle. Our friends, the Schwartzes, have a lot of evergreen trees on their property on Whidbey. Around the holidays they let their friends who celebrate Christmas go to their summer place and chop one down to bring back to the city for a Christmas tree. We've never had one of the Schwartzes' trees. We always get ugly trees from one of the parking lots on Rainier Avenue. But I like to get Charlie Brown trees that are the kind of trees no one would want and then

19

we decorate them all up and make them gorgeous, and the trees are happy that they didn't get left alone forever in the parking lot on Rainier Avenue. But sometimes I think it would be nice to go and chop one down from the Schwartzes. Their summer place is so neat.

One of the best things about it is Helene's horse, Charlie. Today, one thing I am happy about is that I'll probably get to ride him. Charlie's a nice old gray horse with big brown eyes. I used to wish more than anything in the world that Charlie belonged to me and not to Helene Schwartz. But now I have some other things to worry about—like Trae turning beautiful— and I don't think quite as much about Helene getting to have Charlie.

When we got to the Schwartzes', Mom and Sam and Mr. and Mrs. Schwartz all hugged each other and Helene came running up from the barn. She said "Hi" to all of us, but especially to Larry, and then she smiled at him a lot and asked him if he wanted to ride Charlie. She didn't even ask me.

Sara and David wanted to go down to the dock, and Mom said that I had to go down with them to make sure they didn't fall in and drown. I was used to having to watch Sara and make sure that she didn't drown, but now to have to make sure that David didn't drown too was just too much.

"That's not fair! How come Larry gets to go

riding and I get stuck with these two? He should have to watch David and Sara too!''

Mom just looked at Sam like she couldn't figure out what to do, and finally Sam said, ''Cynthia, you and Larry take turns—you watch the kids while Larry has a turn on the horse, and then Larry, you go down to the dock while Cynthia rides.''

I was still mad, but at least I would get a turn on Charlie, so I took Sara and David down to the dock. The tide must have been really high recently because there were a couple of dead little fish on the end of the dock. Sara and David thought this was wonderful and they got some sticks and started poking one. Sara would squeal and then David would say how gushy it was, and I had to listen to all this while I was sitting there watching Larry ride Charlie. Larry was riding all over the place, and Helene was prancing all around Larry as if he were some wonderful person and the greatest rider on earth. I was stuck with two little kids and two smelly dead fish.

Larry rode near the dock and I yelled at him, ''It's my turn, Larry! Get off and come down here!''

Larry smiled and waved to me and pretended he didn't hear me. I just knew he did.

''Larry! GET DOWN HERE—IT'S MY TURN!'' I yelled louder. Larry just smiled and waved some more and went trotting by on

Charlie while Helene kept telling him what a great rider he was.

Then Mrs. Schwartz came out on the porch. "Helene!" she called. "Better head Charlie back to the barn—we're going to eat dinner soon."

Sara and David heard that and ran back up to the house. Larry and Helene headed back to the barn with Charlie. They walked up to the house together.

I sat on the dock and looked at the two dead fish with their glassy eyes staring up at me. I started to cry. I took the stick David had dropped and poked the fish, wiping the tears from my face.

Four

I didn't eat much dessert after dinner, which is not like me. Mom had brought the dessert along with some wine and cheese for the Schwartzes, and the dessert was some wonderful chocolate eclairs from Marcel's pastry shop.

This is usually one of my all-time favorite desserts. But I just sat there and watched everyone else gobble them up. I only ate about half of mine, and after David had eaten three, he asked me if I was going to eat the rest of my eclair. I told him he could have it—but later I wished I had saved it for when I was feeling more like eating. I was too sad to even be mad.

After dinner Sara and David had to clear off the table and Helene and Larry and I had to do the dishes. Helene said for me to wash and she and Larry would dry so she could tell him where to put the stuff away. I would much rather dry than wash, but it was her house, so I didn't say anything. She seemed to like telling Larry which cupboards to put the dishes in, and she kept bumping into him as they put the dishes away—sort of like it was an accident, but I was pretty sure it wasn't. When a person is going to be your brother it's hard to think of him as being a boy—at least the kind of boy a person could like. But Helene was not acting like Larry was a brother.

When we finished the dishes we went out to the field with the soccer ball Larry had brought up with us to Whidbey. Larry always seems to have a soccer ball with him wherever he goes. It looks like it's connected to his foot. He even dribbles it around the house and Mom never says anything about it. But if I ever mess around with any kind of a ball in the house, she always tells me to go outside and play with it. We're all on soccer teams except for Sara.

Well, Helene isn't on a team either, but she can't do any kind of sports except ride Charlie. Although the way Helene is about Charlie, it doesn't really seem like a sport—it's more like having a pet. I still thought it was crummy that I hadn't gotten a chance to ride him, but Helene said I could have the first turn on Sunday if it was a nice day. Helene doesn't think it's good for Charlie to be out in the rain because he is such an old horse. But I'm sure horses don't mind rain, and I think Helene is probably the one that doesn't like it. That's dumb too, because like Sam says, if you mind rain in Seattle you might as well forget about life.

Larry is the goalie on his soccer team. I play striker—that's the one that makes all the goals—and David plays midfield. Larry is on the Slammers, David is on the Bombers, and I am on the Roto Rooters. I wish my team had a good name like theirs, but we are sponsored by our neighborhood Roto Rooter company—they pay for our uniforms and everything—so we have to be named the Roto Rooters. I think that is a really terrible name for a soccer team, and what I hate is some of the things the other teams we play say to us. Like they yell, "Hey Roto Rooters—you sure are crappy!" and also stuff like, "You Roto Rooters belong in the sewer!" and sometimes they even say, "We're going to flush you down the toilet!" and think it's so funny. I don't think it's funny at all.

Sara doesn't like to play soccer much because she is afraid of balls. She wants to be the person who wears the Seahawk costume at football games when she grows up. The Seahawks are the Seattle football team, and the Sounders are the soccer team, but they don't have anything dressed up like an animal. They do have some kids who run around the Sounders games with giant soccer balls over their heads and all that sticks out is their legs.

But Sara says she'd rather be a Seahawk. I think the Seahawks is kind of a funny name for a football team because I don't know anyone in Seattle who has even seen a seahawk—most people don't even know what a seahawk is. We do have a lot of sea gulls around, but I guess the Sea Gulls wouldn't be a very good name for a football team because it doesn't sound tough. But Sara does like to come to all my soccer games and root for the Roto Rooters.

As usual Sara didn't want to play, so she was among the spectators. The teams were David and me against Larry and Helene. We brought the garbage cans around from the side of the house to be the goals. We didn't play with a goalie because even though that's the position that Larry plays on the Slammers it just doesn't work to have a goalie when there are only two people on the team. Also, that would leave only Helene to be the whole rest of the team and that definitely would not be much of a team. She really is ridiculous when she tries to play soccer. She just runs around and squeals and falls down a lot. Usually she doesn't like to play, but she did today because I think she wanted to impress Larry.

David made a goal and I made a goal and Larry made two—so the score was tied 2–2. After Larry's last goal it was our turn to kick off. David put the ball in the middle of the field and passed to me. Helene started squealing, "Get her, Larry—get the ball!" while she just stood there by the garbage can. I guess she was the defense.

But I quickly dribbled away from Larry as he was trying to slide tackle me, and with some of my magnificent footwork I ran like the wind down the field toward the goal. Then I poised for the shot, and because they don't call me Big Foot on the Roto Rooters for nothing, the ball boomed forward like a cannon ball and was heading straight for the goal. Helene just stood there in front of the garbage can like a robot and the ball hit her in the stomach and sent her flying into the garbage can. She ended up sprawled on the grass in the middle of a bunch of empty milk cartons, egg shells, coffee grounds, chicken bones, and a lot of other garbage. She also had the lid partly over her head.

David and Sara thought it was funny and they started laughing hysterically and running around. I couldn't help laughing too—but I was worried that Helene might be hurt. Larry and I went over to the garbage can and took the lid off her head.

"Are you okay?" I asked. "I didn't mean for you to get hurt or anything."

Helene didn't say anything. She just lay there in the middle of the garbage. She looked kind of stunned.

"Maybe we better get Dad," Larry said, looking kind of worried.

I started to go back to the house to get Sam, but just then Helene got up and brushed some of the garbage off of herself and walked back to the house. She didn't say a word to any of us. She held her head up real high as if nothing had bothered her at all—but she looked kind of funny because she had a chicken bone and some egg shells stuck to her hair.

While Helene was in the shower cleaning up after the game and washing the garbage out of her hair, the rest of us played Monopoly. I used to love to play Monopoly with Sara. That's because Sara doesn't know how to add and I got to be banker all the time. I always won. But now that Larry and David play with us, I don't get to be banker all the time because Larry knows how to add. I don't always win anymore.

Sara and David were getting bored playing Monopoly and they wanted to stop. David said he wanted all of us to put on a play for the parents. Sara thought that was a great idea and she wanted to do "Goldilocks and the Three Bears," which is a play she had been in at the Peace and Freedom nursery school a few years ago. I thought I was too old to be in "Goldilocks and the Three Bears," but Larry said it was okay with him as long as we would all be in another skit that he knew about from camp. I said I'd go see if Helene was done in the shower and find out if it was okay with her.

I went upstairs to the bathroom and knocked on the door.

"Helene?" I asked. "Are you out of the shower—can I come in?"

"Sure—just a second." Helene unlocked the door and let me in. The Schwartzes really had a nice bathroom for a summer place. It had a pink bath carpet on the floor and a nice sink that was set in a long counter top. I sat up on the counter top and Helene plugged in the blow dryer and was drying her hair.

"You really have pretty hair, Helene," I said. I was still feeling kind of bad that I had knocked her into the garbage.

"Well, it looks a lot better when it doesn't have chicken bones in it," she said, laughing. "I am just not cut out to be a soccer player, I guess."

"I'm really sorry that happened."

"Well, I know you didn't mean for me to end up in the garbage . . . I wonder what Larry thinks?"

"Larry?"

"Yeah . . . he sure is cute. You are really lucky that he's going to be your stepbrother."

"You think so?"

"Of course! Do you think he likes me?"

"You mean for a girlfriend?"

"Well, yeah, sort of—I mean what does he think about me—has he ever said anything?"

"I really don't know—I don't know if Larry even likes girls—I never talk to him about stuff like that."

"Oh—well could you find out for me—you know—just sort of casually ask him what he thinks about me and be sure and tell him that I really think he's nice and cute too. Okay?"

"I guess so . . . listen, they're all sick of playing Monopoly, and Sara and David want all of us to put on a play for the parents—do you want to? I said I'd come up here and ask you."

"Does Larry want to?"

"He said he would if we would all do a skit that he did at camp."

"Oh well, in that case, sure—I'd love to. What are we supposed to do?"

"Well, the little kids want to do 'Goldilocks and the Three Bears'—I know that sounds dumb—but I'm not sure what Larry's skit is."

"Well, that's okay, it doesn't matter . . . all I know is that I sure don't want to play soccer again." Helene finished drying her hair and we went into the bedroom while she got dressed. I didn't mean to notice her so much while she was getting dressed, but it was hard not to. I was sitting on the bed and trying to look at the pattern in the bedspread, but I kept looking at her. She was definitely getting a body, and what was worse than that, she put on a bra. I was feeling kind of dumb sitting there in my jeans and T-shirt with nothing under the T-shirt but me.

"Do you have one yet?" she asked, hooking up her bra.

"No."

"Oh that's too bad. Well, I got mine a few months ago—it's really a kind of training bra."

"Training for what?"

"Oh just getting used to having straps and elastic around you—so your body gets in training for that."

"Oh." I didn't say anything, but I wondered why a person's body needed to get trained to have elastic on it.

"Cynthia, you really should have your mother get you a training bra—I mean we are in the sixth grade."

"Well, I don't know. I'm hoping I won't grow because it might mess up gymnastics for me." Actually I lied about that, but as long as you are one of just a few people who are the no-bra people you might as well have an important reason for not wanting to grow and just pretend that you don't care about all that.

"What does needing a bra have to do with gymnastics?"

"Well, you can just be a much better gymnast if you stay short and also stay flat. Everyone knows that. Even in the newspapers they're saying that the Russians give the girls on their team some drugs to make them stay little so they can win medals.''

"Well, personally, I'd rather wear a bra than win a medal.''

"Not me," I said, as if I were very sure about that.

"Those Russians—do they get their period?''

"I don't know.''

"Well, that would really be dumb to take drugs so you never need a bra and then you don't even get your period.''

"Do you have yours yet?'' I asked.

"No—but I expect it any day.''

"Oh.'' I wasn't sure how Helene knew she was expecting her period any day, but I didn't ask her about that because I didn't want to seem too dumb. But it's bad enough to have Trae being one of the bra people in our class. And now to have Helene Schwartz of all people, who not only has a horse and seems to be in love with my stepbrother, also to have a bra—even if she calls it a training bra, which I think is ridiculous, is just too much.

Helene finished getting dressed and we went down to get ready for the play and Larry's skit. "Don't forget to ask Larry about me—okay?'' she whispered as we walked into the kitchen. I said I would, and then we sat down at the kitchen table with Larry, David, and Sara.

They were making bears' heads out of grocery bags for the costumes for the play.

"I'm Goldilocks," Sara said, "and Larry is Papa Bear and David is Baby Bear—will you be Mama Bear, Cynthia?"

"Sure—but what about Helene?"

"She can be the narrator," Larry said. "You know, she can say 'Once upon a time . . .' and stuff like that."

"I know—I'll go get a book and I'll sit there and pretend I'm reading from it."

Helene went to find a big book, and I made a bear's head out of a grocery bag, the same way Sara had made hers. We taped on some ears and cut holes out of the bag for eyes and nose and a mouth. Then we colored around the eyes and the mouth. We all tried on our bags and they looked pretty good. The play wasn't hard and the only thing Larry had to say was "Someone's been sitting in my chair," and the only thing I had to say was "Someone's been eating my porridge," and the only thing David had to say was "Someone's been lying in my bed, and there she is!" We all practiced it a few times. Sara got a mop to put on her head to be Goldilocks.

I thought Larry's skit was kind of stupid, but Helene acted like it was the funniest thing she had ever seen. Larry stood on a chair and Sara sat on it with her feet showing. Helene held a blanket that showed Sara's feet but covered

Larry all up except for his head. It made him look like he was about six feet tall. Then I come in and see Larry standing there and say to him, "Why are you so tall?" and Larry says, "I greased myself and I greased myself and I greased myself, until I got taller and taller and taller." Then David comes in and says, "I greased myself too, but it didn't work." Then Larry says, "Did you grease behind your ears and between your toes?" Then David says, "No, I'll try that." And he leaves and when he comes back in, he crawls on his knees and says, "I greased myself everywhere but it doesn't work. I'm just getting shorter." Then I'm supposed to say to David, "Well, what did you use?" and then David says "Crisco," and then Larry says, "Well, of course, that doesn't work—that's shortening." And that's the end of the skit.

Helene told Larry it was just wonderful and that everyone would really think it was great. So we practiced it a bunch of times. We decided to do Larry's skit first and end with "The Three Bears." Sara was excited about getting everyone to do her play—it was very important to her since we hardly ever do any of Sara's ideas about anything.

Larry and I went and told the parents that we were going to put on plays and for them to sit in the living room. We did Larry's skit first and it went fine and everyone laughed when

Larry said, "Well, of course, that doesn't work—that's shortening!" although I still thought it was kind of dumb.

Then it was time to do "The Three Bears." We all put the grocery bags on our heads in the kitchen and waited for Helene to start telling the story. She was sitting by the fireplace in the living room—pretending to read the story from the book. We got through the play fine, until it was time for David, who was Baby Bear, to say, "Someone's been sleeping in my bed, and there she is!" But what happened was that David ruined the whole play. Sara was lying on some pillows that were supposed to be a bed with a mop on her head, and David came in and looked at Sara. He started giggling under his grocery bag and couldn't stop.

Sara sat up and took the mop off her head and threw it down. The parents started clapping anyway because I guess they thought that was the end of the play. Sara was so mad. "Listen, David," she said, "just because my mother is getting married to your father doesn't mean that you have to ruin the whole play!"

Five

On the way home from Whidbey I remembered I had promised Helene I'd ask Larry what he thinks about her. I didn't especially want to do anything for her because I never did get to ride Charlie. Besides that, having Helene make such a big deal about Larry is not all that much fun for me. But I asked him anyway. We were in the car on the way to Larry and David's house. Sam was going to drop them off on the way back to our house.

"Larry—what do you think of Helene? She thinks you're really cute and nice."

"Helene?" Larry mumbled like he was kind of embarrassed.

"Yeah, Helene Schwartz—the person we just spent the whole weekend with who was chasing you around the whole time?" Boys act so dumb sometimes. I mean Larry sounded like he didn't know which Helene I was talking about.

"Oh yeah—that Helene," he mumbled.

"Well, what do you think about that Helene?" I was wishing I had never promised her I would even ask him. Larry acts so strange about girls. I can't figure that out either because along with a bunch of posters of Pelé and people like that, and some football players, Larry also has a poster of a movie star and she is wearing a too-small bathing suit.

"She's okay, I guess."

That was the end of the conversation because we got to Larry and David's house and dropped them off.

When we got home I went right up to my room to see if my animals were still alive and to check over my room to make sure Harry hadn't been messing in any of my stuff. The animals seemed to be okay, and I was going through my drawers and my closet, when the phone rang. Mom answered it from the kitchen and yelled up that it was for me. I love getting phone calls. I went in my mom's room and picked up the phone.

"Hello."

"Hi, Cynthia—it's Helene. Did you ask him?"

"Oh yeah—on the way home in the car."

"Well, what did he say—tell me everything!" Helene said excitedly.

"Well, I asked him what he thought of you and I told him that you thought he was really cute and nice."

"And then what—what did Larry say?"

"He said that you were okay."

"That's all! That's all he said?"

"I think so."

"Well, tell me exactly—what were his exact words?"

"His exact words were 'she's okay, I guess.' "

"Well—do you think he likes me, Cynthia?"

"How should I know?—I mean that's all he said, Helene, and I don't know if he likes you."

"He's going to be your stepbrother and everything, I mean, I would think you would know him pretty well by now."

"Larry and I never talk about stuff like that."

"You sure are lucky to have such a fox for a brother. How often do you get to see him?"

"Larry and David usually come every weekend. But some weekends Sara and I aren't here because we're at my dad's apartment."

"Well, listen, Cynthia, the next weekend that Larry comes, I want to come over, if you're not at your dad's."

"You know somehow I get the idea that you don't just want to see me," I said. I was getting mad.

"Don't be silly. I'd never come over to see

38

Larry if you weren't there. I like to do stuff with you. And for sure you can ride Charlie the next time you come up to Whidbey."

"I have to get off the phone, Helene."

"Why? Does your mother have to use it or something?"

"No—I have to go and spray my room."

"Spray your room?"

"Yeah, that's what I said, I have to go and spray my room with air deodorant because Harry Z fed my animals while we were at Whidbey this weekend, and I have to get rid of the Harry Z germs. Bye, Helene." I hung up.

I got the air-freshener stuff and ran all over my room spraying it with lemon-lime-pine scent. But I sprayed too much, and had to open some windows because I was starting to have trouble breathing. I discovered that too much lemon-lime-pine is not good for a person.

After I had sprayed my room to get rid of all Harry Z odor, I called Trae to see how her weekend was. At least she didn't have a crush on Larry.

Mrs. Kaplan answered the phone and I asked to speak with Trae.

"Hi, Cynthia," Trae said. "How was your weekend? When did you get back?"

"We got back about an hour ago and the weekend was mostly not good."

"Really? What happened?"

"Oh, Helene fell in the garbage can while we

were playing soccer. I was worried that she got hurt but she was just mad. Then mostly she just chased Larry around. I think she likes him.''

"For a boyfriend?'' Trae asked.

"Yeah. And then Sara got mad at David because he ruined her play that we put on for the parents, and also I never did get to ride Charlie.''

"That's usually the best part about going up to the Schwartzes,'' Trae said.

"Yeah, I know. How was your weekend?''

"Well—it was okay, but I sure wish you had been here. I walked the dog down to the park on Saturday, and Richie Hinkley was playing baseball with some guys in our class, and he talked to me a lot and even started playing baseball with me. It was wonderful—you should have been here!''

"You don't even like baseball, Trae.''

"I'd like anything with Richie Hinkley—he was showing me how to throw the ball and catch it and stuff like that.''

"Oh.''

"Listen, do you want to walk down to Pay 'n Save with me? I want to get some fingernail polish and look at the records.''

"I guess so—but I'll have to ask Mom.''

"Okay—call me back if you can.''

"All right—bye.'' I hung up the phone and went in the bathroom and looked in the mirror. Why couldn't I look like Trae? She doesn't even like baseball or soccer or anything like that. She's not even on the Roto Rooters . . . and she gets Richie Hinkley, the cutest boy in our class, to teach her how to throw. It's so unfair!

I stared at my face in the mirror and wondered if I really was that ugly. I started combing my hair and parting it a different way and trying to see if I could get it to look better when I noticed some red bumps on my face. I looked more closely in the mirror. I really did have some strange red bumps. One was on my forehead and another on the end of my nose. They didn't itch, so I didn't think they were bug bites—but I wondered if maybe I was getting the measles or something like that. I went down to the kitchen to ask Mom about it. Also Sam might know what was the matter because he's a doctor. Mom was making dinner. Sara had gone to the store with Sam to get some milk. I hoped they would get some more Doritos too, since Larry and David had eaten them all up.

"There's something weird on my face, Mom."

She looked at my forehead and my nose and said, "Cynthia, honey, those are pimples— that's all—nothing to worry about. You're just growing up."

"You're sure I don't have the measles or a rash?"

"No, just pimples—nothing to worry about— just wash your face real well and it will be all right. People usually just get pimples when they start growing up—that's all.''

I went back up to my room and closed the door. I was so mad. Here my mother is saying I'm growing up and all it's about is pimples. When Helene and Trae and people like that are growing up, they get to wear a bra and are expecting their period any day and stuff like that, and what do I get? Pimples!

I didn't really feel like going to Pay 'n Save with Trae who has no pimples. I didn't feel like much of anything. This growing up business was not happening the way I planned it. But finally I decided that it wasn't Trae's fault that I had these pimples growing on my face, and I went back downstairs to ask Mom if I could go. Mom said I could.

''Cynthia, here's some money. When you're at Pay 'n Save, pick up a tube of Clearasil—it's something to put on your pimples that will probably get rid of them faster.'' She gave me a hug and said for me to be sure and be back before dinner.

I felt better that Mom had given me some money to get some pimple stuff, but I still wish that the first thing I bought having to do with being a teen-ager was about underwear and not pimple junk.

Trae and I walked past Mount Baker Park on the way to Pay 'n Save, and Richie Hinkley was out there playing baseball. He waved to

Trae, but acted like I wasn't even there. Then she talked all about him the whole way down McClellan to Rainier Avenue. She kept talking about how cute he was and how she had so much fun with him on Saturday. When we got to Pay 'n Save, I looked around the store and wandered around by where they had the pimple stuff. I just didn't feel like buying it. Trae was looking at fingernail polish and she bought some called "Red Hot Mama," which was real dark red. I bite my fingernails sometimes and I don't have much to polish, so I didn't buy any.

But I did find a small diary over in the stationery section. It was light blue and it had a little lock on it with a key taped to the inside. I wanted it so much, I decided to buy it with the money Mom had given me for the pimple stuff. I was sure Mom wouldn't mind. It was getting hard these days to find anyone to talk to, so I decided it would be good to have a diary to write down my most private things and personal business in.

It was dinner time when I got home, and Mom and Sam were talking about the wedding and their honeymoon. They were going to take the train up to Vancouver, B.C., and then take a ferry to Victoria. They would stay in the Empress Hotel. We went there once a long time ago when Mom was still married to my dad. It is a huge old-fashioned hotel, and it has a big lobby with old furniture all over the place, and they serve tea in the lobby every afternoon. It is very, very English, and all the people seem English even though it is in Canada. I love the Empress.

Sara and I have to have great Aunt Gertrude come and stay with us while Mom and Sam are on their honeymoon, and I know that will not be wonderful. But at least the wedding part should be pretty good. At dinner I asked my mother about the wedding—about when I would get my wonderful dress and the body permanent and the basket full of rose petals to scatter over the heads of all the hundreds of people who would be there.

"Cynthia," she said, "only the relatives are coming. The wedding is in the living room, and we have to clean the cat stains off the rug."

Six

I spent the weekend before the wedding trying to clean the cat stains off the rug instead of getting a body permanent. It wasn't a very good weekend, except that Sara and I did get to go out with Dad on Sunday night. He had called and said that he wanted to take us out to dinner because he was going to be out of town the weekend of the wedding and would be traveling on business for a few weeks after that.

My father travels a lot for his business. He is the Northwest Manager for the Bluewater Boat Company, which is a company that makes sailboats. My father loves sailing and he especially likes racing and being in the big sailboat races. My mom is so different about that. She always thought that sailing was best if you would just be relaxed and cruise around and not be in a hurry to go anywhere. My dad likes to be in races and go fast and try hard to be the best and beat everyone and win the race. Not only were they different about sailing, but they were different about almost everything else. I sure hope Mom and Sam don't turn out to be like that.

Dad said we could pick the restaurant where we wanted to eat, and Sara and I picked the top of the Space Needle. But Daddy said that was too much money, so we picked the Old Spaghetti Factory.

When Dad came to pick us up, he rang the doorbell and Sara let him in. When my parents were first divorced, it used to seem so strange to have him come over and ring the doorbell, because he used to live here. But he hasn't lived with us for a long time, and now it doesn't seem strange when he rings the doorbell. Sam was there when Dad came. He walked over to my father and they shook hands.

"Hi, Sam, how are you?" Dad asked, shaking Sam's hand.

"Fine, Dan, how are you?" Sam was very polite. They are both always very polite, but about all they ever say to each other is stuff like that, and sometimes something about how the weather has been lately.

Sara and I left with Dad and drove to the Old Spaghetti Factory. It doesn't take reservations and you always have to wait in line for a long time to get a table.

Dad parked the car and we walked in and went to the desk and Dad gave them our names.

"A table for three," he said to the lady, "the name is Browne."

"We'll have a table for you in about thirty-five minutes," the lady said, writing down our name.

"You don't have anything any sooner?" Daddy sounded kind of mad.

"I'm sorry, sir, that's the earliest time we'll have one available."

Daddy asked Sara and me if we'd like to go somewhere else. He suggested McDonald's. But Sara and I didn't want to—we always go to McDonald's and it is not special, and this dinner out was supposed to be special. It had started out to be the top of the Space Needle, and then it had turned into the Old Spaghetti Factory, and now it looked like it might turn into McDonald's. This dinner was going downhill fast. McDonald's is for when your mother is too tired to cook.

Sara and I told him that we didn't mind waiting and that we really wanted to eat at the Old Spaghetti Factory, so Dad finally said we could stay. But he didn't seem happy about it. In fact, he seemed unusually grumpy to me. He sat down in one of the chairs and smoked a lot of cigarettes while Sara and I walked around and looked at all the neat stuff they have. At the Old Spaghetti Factory they have an old-fashioned player piano, and if you put in fifty cents it plays music all by itself. Sara went over to where Dad was sitting and asked him for fifty cents so she could make the piano play all by itself.

"No, Sara—it's just a waste of money. Somebody will probably play it anyway if you just wait, and then you can watch how it works without losing fifty cents."

"Okay," Sara said, walking back over to the piano, but she seemed disappointed. I think if Dad had been in a better mood he might have given Sara the fifty cents. But he definitely was in a bad mood tonight.

Finally the lady called our name. "The Browne party of three," she said real loud.

"It's about time," Daddy muttered, walking over to Sara and me where we were waiting by the player piano, hoping someone would come along and put fifty cents in.

"Come on, girls," Dad said, motioning for us to follow him, "our table's ready." Just then a man came up to the piano and put in fifty cents.

"Wait, Daddy," Sara said, jumping up and down, "I want to see the piano work!"

"Dammit, Sara, come on. We've been waiting around to eat at this place all night and

I'm not going to wait any longer than I have to."

Dad followed the lady with the menus into the restaurant part and Sara and I followed him. We didn't talk much. The lady showed us to a regular, ordinary table and we all sat down. I was hoping that we might get to eat inside the old railroad car that they have right inside the restaurant, but we didn't have any luck about that. We never got to see the piano work, either.

A man came and took our order. We all had the same thing—spaghetti, garlic bread, and salad, except that Sara and I had Cokes and Dad had some wine.

So far with this dinner out with our dad, the only good part was that Ellen didn't come along. Ellen is my father's girl friend and I like being with my dad alone a lot better than I like it with her around. I don't hate her the way I used to, but I still like being with Dad alone the best.

"Well, girls," Daddy said, rolling his spaghetti on his fork, "I leave tomorrow for Portland, San Francisco, and then I'll be going down to Los Angeles. I should be gone almost three weeks. We have a lot of business in California this time of year."

"Does that mean you'll be gone when Mom and Sam are away on their honeymoon?" I asked.

"Yes, Cynthia. I'll be out of town the whole time. Ellen is going with me, and we thought we might spend a few days just relaxing around Carmel and Monterey so it won't be all business."

"Couldn't you go some other time?" I was worried, and I didn't like the idea of having no parents at all left in Seattle.

"No, this is the time I need to get away," Dad said, and he sounded kind of strange, almost sad. "Isn't great Aunt Gertrude going to stay with you?"

"Yuk," Sara said, slurping up her spaghetti, "yuk—great Aunt Gertrude—yuk."

"Sara, don't talk with your mouth full," Dad said.

"Yeah, she's going to stay with us—but Sara and I don't like her." I thought about asking him again to change his mind and stay in town while Mom and Sam were away. But I could tell that I wouldn't get anywhere with that at all. He was just acting too grumpy and sad too.

We didn't talk much on the way home from the Old Spaghetti Factory, and I was thinking about how Dad was acting. I wondered if it had anything to do with Mom getting married and going away on her honeymoon.

"Dad? Do you have to go away on this trip right now because of the wedding and the honeymoon?"

"Something like that, although I really do have a lot of business to take care of." After he said that he turned on the radio, and I could tell he didn't want to talk about it anymore.

When we got home, Dad kissed Sara and me and said that he would see us in about three weeks. I wished so much that he had stayed around to be with us instead of great Aunt Gertrude, because if there ever was a time I thought I needed him, it was now.

I started thinking about why he had seemed so grumpy and sad. It was hard to figure out because Dad and Mom got a divorce because they didn't want to be married to each other, so why should he care that she got married again. Also, he had Ellen, and he was taking her on the business trip.

The only thing I could ever figure out that might be like how Dad was acting had to do with a cat that I used to have. I had it a long time ago before I got Martha. I loved this cat when it was a kitten, but then later it was a whole bunch of trouble.

All cats are supposed to automatically know about going in a litter box. But this was a very dumb cat. It never did get the idea, and because my mom said I was in charge of this cat, I had to spend all this time all over the house cleaning up cat messes. This cat thought it was supposed to go in the plants and under the dining room table and behind the living room couch. It especially thought it was supposed to go in my room. The cat thought my whole room was a litter box. I hated the cat messes more than I loved the cat. So finally, I gave it away. I had a friend in my class named Shelly who took the cat, and even though I didn't want it anymore, somehow when I knew it belonged to Shelly and not to me, I felt sad. Shelly loved cats and I knew she would be good to it, but it also kind of made me mad.

Besides not having my father be in town while Mom and Sam went on their honeymoon, the wedding also did not turn out the way I planned. There wasn't even a real minister. He turned out to be an ex-minister who was a friend of my mother and Sam. He was a real estate salesman who used to be a minister, and he read from a book called *The Prophet,* and my mother and Sam didn't even say, "I do."

They made up their own stuff to say, and it was not like the weddings on TV at all. The hundreds of people I had planned on turned out to be my Gramma and Grampa from Denver, my Uncle Melvin, the psychiatrist, and Aunt Bonnye, Uncle Peter and Aunt Artis, Aunt Rosetta and Uncle Bill, Uncle Joey and Aunt Vera, and then my new aunts and uncles from Sam's family. I guess they are really step-aunts and stepuncles; they were Uncle Len and

Aunt Dorothy, Uncle Bob and Aunt Betty, Uncle Jack and Aunt Shirley, and Uncle Dexter and Aunt Virginia. Of course great Aunt Gertrude was there too. The only people who weren't the relatives were Constance and Norman Schwartz.

We had a lot of candles and flowers in the living room, and the relatives all stood around, and I don't think anyone noticed the cat stains on the rug that never did come out.

But I did get to be in the wedding and so did Sara and Larry and David. Our part was giving the wedding rings to my mother and Sam. We sat next to them during the wedding and before it, too, when my Gramma from Denver played the piano.

Sara and I wore some dresses that kind of looked like dresses from *Little House on the Prairie*. The dress was okay, but it wasn't at all what I had in mind when I thought that I was going to be the star of my mother's wedding.

One thing that happened was that David got the ring box stuck to his tie. It snapped on his tie and he sat there the whole time like that, with this dumb box on his tie.

After the wedding, Aunt Vera and Uncle Joey gave us some champagne especially for kids. It was supposed to taste like real champagne. We all liked it except for Sara. She ran out of the wedding and spit it out in the bath-room.

It really wasn't a terrible wedding after all, but it was still not the wedding I planned. But later what turned out to be really awful was the honeymoon.

Seven

The honeymoon was crummy because I didn't get to go. Not only that, it just seemed like everything went wrong. Mom was gone, Sam was gone, my dad was gone, Larry and David were with their mother, and the only family I had left to be with was Sara, great Aunt Gertrude, and my animals.

I had gotten most of my animals during our divorce. Harry Z had told me that when parents get divorced, sometimes they feel bad about it and so they buy you a bunch of stuff and take you places. He said they do this to make up for the divorce and show you that they love you. That was one of the few things that Harry had ever been right about. I have always loved animals. In addition to Martha, my cat, I was able to get Mildred, my canary, Ernie and Burt, the two hamsters which were from Harry because he found out he was allergic, my fish, and also my guinea pig, Howard.

Mostly I would be talking to my mother about missing Daddy, and then I would ask her about having this bird or the hamsters, and she would say okay, that I could get them. I loved having the animals in my room, and they were no problem at all, except, of course, when we all went out of town and I had to get Harry to feed them. Except for that, about the only thing I had to remember was to keep Martha locked in the closet while I let Ernie and Burt and Howard run around the room. Martha also had to be in the closet when I let Mildred out of her bird cage to fly around the room to get some exercise.

The only kind of animal Sara ever really wanted was a monkey. Then after Mom and Dad were divorced and Dad was taking us to the zoo so much, she got interested in gorillas because they are bigger.

Right before the honeymoon Sara came in my room while I was playing with my animals. Sara watched while Mildred was flying around getting exercise. Martha was locked in the closet and Howard and Ernie and Burt were out of their cages running around too.

"Cynthia, I think I'd really like to have a gorilla—do you think Mom would get me one?"

I was sure no one ever had a gorilla outside

of a zoo, so I said to Sara, "No, but you could try for a monkey."

"How should I ask her? Should I just say, 'Hey, Mom, how 'bout a monkey?' "

"No, Sara. What you do is say something about the divorce, and then about Sam and the honeymoon and say that you miss Daddy—then ask for the monkey."

My mother was in the middle of packing and Sam was gone getting plane tickets and stopping by Larry and David's house to say good-bye. Mom was making all kinds of lists for great Aunt Gertrude when Sara walked into the bedroom.

Sara went up to Mom and said, "Mom—about the divorce—I'd like a monkey."

"Sara, this place has already turned into a complete zoo—great Aunt Gertrude is coming and now you want a monkey! That's ridiculous. We are not having a monkey!"

Mom went on packing and making her lists, and Sara came into my room and started yelling at me. She said I told her the wrong thing to say to Mom and that's why she couldn't have the monkey, and it wasn't fair, and it was all my fault, and then she threw a big handful of birdseed all over my room and ran out, slamming the door.

I got mad at that birdseed all over my room, and I ran after Sara. "You come back here right now, you little creep, and pick up every seed of this birdseed!'' I screamed. She had locked herself in the bathroom, and I started pounding on the door, calling her names that I can't mention here.

My mother came and said, ''What's going on with you girls?''

Then the doorbell rang, and great Aunt Gertrude was there with her suitcase. Mom let her in while I was pounding the door to the bathroom and screaming at Sara.

My mother told great Aunt Gertrude to just sit down and make herself comfortable, that the girls were just having a little argument and not to worry about it. Then she came upstairs, and I knew we were really going to get it.

When my mother is really, really mad she talks through her teeth and squinches up her eyes and her face gets maroon and her jaw muscles start twitching. That's the way she looked now, and she said in this absolutely deadly whisper, ''Sara . . . come out . . . now.''

Sara unlocked the door and came out.

Then she said, ''Cynthia . . . get the vacuum cleaner . . . now.''

I got the vacuum cleaner.

She said in this horrible whisper so great Aunt Gertrude wouldn't hear, ''I do not care who started what. You will each take turns and vacuum up the birdseed. Cynthia, all the animals will be in their cages, and you are NEVER to use those words in front of great Aunt Gertrude or—'' Then she said in this really scary voice, ''Great Aunt Gertrude will be in her grave!''

Sara started vacuuming. I put the animals in their cages, and then I vacuumed some, and we didn't say a word to each other for a long time. Martha was still locked in the closet, and the only noise was Martha meowing because she doesn't like the vacuum cleaner.

''Cynthia, you know what I can't figure out?''

''What?''

I kept vacuuming up the birdseed while Sara picked it out of the corners of the room where the vacuum couldn't get it.

''I can't figure out how come great Aunt Gertrude will be in her grave because I threw birdseed in your room.''

I couldn't figure it out either, but because I am supposed to know more than Sara I just said, ''Well, it's not only that, it's just that Mom's afraid that we'll freak out great Aunt Gertrude or something.''

''Well, I'm afraid we'll get freaked out by great Aunt Gertrude,'' Sara said, throwing a big handful of birdseed in my wastebasket. Sara and I didn't know it then, but she turned out to be exactly right.

Great Aunt Gertrude doesn't know anything about kids. She thinks girls should wear dresses to school. And the whole time of the honey-moon she kept bugging me and Sara to wear dresses. Great Aunt Gertrude said that jeans are what you should change into after school. No one in my entire class, in fact no girl in our entire school, wears a dress. Except for Rose-mary Babcock, who has real leather boots and a longish skirt that she wears a lot and thinks looks wonderful. But she is the only one. Everyone else wears pants. I don't even have a dress that fits anymore, except for that Little House on the Prairie dress that Mom bought me for the wedding. I told this to great Aunt Gertrude, but what she did was to go downtown on the bus to Frederick and Nelson's and buy two ugly dresses—one for me and one for Sara—and said we had to wear them to school and be young ladies.

Sara didn't mind, but when I tried to tell great Aunt Gertrude that no one wears dresses ex-cept for Rosemary Babcock who has leather boots to go with it, she said, "Cynthia, just because you're from a broken home doesn't mean that you can't look like a young lady."

That's what she kept saying over and over the whole honeymoon—all this stuff about a broken home. I guess a broken home is how old people call a divorce. Like every time I would say to Sara, "Up your nose with a rubber hose," and Sara would say to me, "Get off my case, toilet face" (which we say to each other all the time, and everyone in my school has been saying to each other for years), great Aunt Gertrude would say, "Just because you girls are from a broken home doesn't mean you have to say those terrible things."

I got so sick of her bothering me about wearing a dress that one day I just wore the stupid dress, even if I didn't have any leather boots like Rosemary Babcock. It was a big mistake.

The morning I had to wear the dress to school I called Trae. We always call each other in the morning just to talk about what we're wearing that day, and then we meet at the corner, which is halfway between her house and my house. We always meet at the corner every morning at the same time, but we always call just to check anyway. I called Trae from my mom's bedroom so great Aunt Gertrude wouldn't hear. She was down in the kitchen trying to get Sara to eat Cream of Wheat, which Sara hates.

"Hi, Trae—guess what—I have to wear a dress today. Great Aunt Gertrude went down to Fredericks on the bus and bought this ugly dress for me, and she says I have to wear it."

"Do you have any boots?"

"No. The only shoes I have to go with it are either my clogs or my Adidas. What do you think I should do?"

"Well, let's see—the Adidas would look terrible. Better wear the clogs. You know, if we had known sooner, you could have brought

61

some clothes over to my house and then just stopped here to get your clothes. Then if we got to school early, you could have changed in the girls' bathroom. Then you could have stopped at my house on the way home and changed back into the dress. But it's too late now.''

''Yeah, I know. I wish I could be sick today and just stay home. But it's too late for that too. Usually when I want to be sick I have to plan it the night before and not eat and act miserable and start coughing a lot.''

''Well, just wear your coat all day—that might help a little bit. We better leave now though 'cause it's almost eight-thirty.''

''Okay, see you at the corner.''

I put on my coat and left the house. It really didn't help at all because it's just a short windbreaker and doesn't cover the skirt of the dress. The whole way to Trae's house I kept thinking about how much I hate great Aunt Gertrude.

Trae and I walked to school together and planned out how I could leave some clothes at her house the whole time great Aunt Gertrude would be staying with us. I thought that was a great idea.

The minute we got to school and walked into class, Stanley Greenstein, a person who Trae and I think is the class turkey, says in front of everyone in this loud yukky voice, ''Well, look at Cynthia, she's trying to look like a girl! Too bad she didn't make it—Ha-ha-ha-ha!''

I have not been in a fight since I was in the fourth grade. Mostly when I think about boys now, I think about which ones are cute and stuff like that. But when Stanley said that, everyone laughed. It is hard enough having the only thing about being a teenager be a few pimples, and then to have your mother gone on her honeymoon and your father gone because of your mother's honeymoon *and* great Aunt Gertrude—well, it was just too much.

I punched out Stanley Greenstein in front of the whole class. His glasses broke and blood started dripping from his nose.

Mrs. Namura, our teacher, pulled me away from Stanley. "Cynthia Browne," she said in this shocked voice, "you come with me."

I ended up in the principal's office and they called great Aunt Gertrude and made her come to school. I was suspended for fighting for the rest of the day. It was awful. I was sitting there in this gross dress with Stanley Greenstein's blood on it and crying. I wasn't crying because Stanley hurt me. That creep didn't even land one punch. I was crying about everything.

I wanted Mom and Sam, and I was worried that something might happen to them, and that they might not come back, and my dad was gone, and I had pimples and no bra, and Trae was beautiful and I wasn't, and Sara and I

weren't allowed even to say "Up your nose
with a rubber hose," and Stanley's mother,
Mrs. Greenstein, was there yelling about
"there's no protection for children in this
school," meaning Stanley, and all dumb great
Aunt Gertrude can say over and over again is
all that stuff about a broken home.

When I got home great Aunt Gertrude made
me go to my room. That was fine with me. I let
all the animals out of their cages and locked
Martha in the closet. But I guess I didn't shut
the closet door good enough because, somehow, Martha got out.

What happened next was so awful that it's
hard to tell about even. Martha got out of the
closet and started chasing the hamsters and she
caught Ernie. Then Mildred flew in the fish
tank. I started running around trying to get
Ernie away from Martha, but it was too late.
Then I ran to the fish tank and I got Mildred
out. But she got pneumonia and died, and Ernie
was dead too.

I just sat there . . . kind of staring at them
and I felt dead too. Then I cried again, and I
was crying and crying when Sara finally came
in my room and found me with dead Ernie and
dead Mildred.

Sara cried too, and we both said how much
we hated great Aunt Gertrude. We made plans
for the funerals for Mildred and Ernie. Sara
asked great Aunt Gertrude if I could come out

of my room so we could have the funerals and bury them in the backyard. Great Aunt Gertrude said okay, and so we buried them next to the white rat we had, which died a year ago.

When we got back in the house, great Aunt Gertrude said that just because we had a broken home we shouldn't have all those animals.

Sara said, "Up your nose with a broken home!"

Eight

When Mom and Sam came back from the honeymoon, I was never so glad in my whole life to see anybody—or so glad to see anybody leave as great Aunt Gertrude. We didn't send her to her grave, but she sent Ernie and Mildred to their graves, and I think she is a completely terrible person.

I wrote a lot about great Aunt Gertrude in my diary while Mom and Sam were on the honeymoon. In fact my diary seemed to be turning into a hate book. I had a whole page for things I hate, and great Aunt Gertrude was at the top of the list. It went like this:

THINGS I HATE

1. *Great Aunt Gertrude*
2. *Trae (for being beautiful), but not all the time because she is my best friend*
3. *pimples*
4. *Harry Z*
5. *no bra*
6. *Stanley Greenstein*
7. *Stanley Greenstein's mother*

My diary wasn't entirely a hate book though, because I was also writing in it some happy things, like being excited about going to camp. This would be my second summer at Happy Hollow Camp, which is in the Cascade Mountains about an hour away from Seattle. I love Happy Hollow. Sara isn't old enough to go yet, but she'll get to go in a few years. It is a girls' and a boys' camp, and they have horses, sailing, swimming, arts and crafts, drama, hiking, tents in the woods that you sleep in, and good food. The counselors are pretty nice too. They are in college, and they sleep in the tents with the kids.

My favorite counselor from last year was a girl named Cordie Underwood. She was very tall and all the kids called her "Long Underwear," but she didn't mind. She was really fun and she seemed to love us very much. But at the end of camp last year, she said she wasn't coming back. She never said why, but all the kids at camp found out that she got fired from being a counselor because the camp director found out she had smoked pot in the bushes near the corral while we were out riding with the riding counselor. I didn't think it was such a big deal, and I was sad that she wouldn't be there this year.

School was out and my friends would all be doing different things this summer. I was going to Happy Hollow, Trae was going to spend the summer in Boise, Idaho, with her grandparents, Richie Hinkley was going to Lenny Wilkens' Basketball Camp, Helene Schwartz was spending the summer at Whidbey Island, Shelly Mahoney was visiting her aunt in Boston, and Harry Zimmerman was taking lessons.

Harry always takes lessons in the summer, depending on what Mrs. Zimmerman thinks is important each year. Last year he took French, the year before that he took violin, and this year he was taking Young People's Personal Growth and Slavic Folk Dancing. Those are two separate lessons. I guess Mrs. Zimmerman thought two things were important this year. Harry is not too happy about it, because he really wants to go to Lenny Wilkens' Basketball Camp with Richie Hinkley. That really would be a waste of Mrs. Zimmerman's money though, because Harry is practically a midget. I think he should go to the Seattle Sounders'

Soccer Camp the way Larry and David are doing, because you can still be practically a midget and play soccer.

Before I went to camp I had to go to the doctor for my camp physical, and also the dentist for my checkup, and this year there was something extra. I had to go to the orthodontist because Dr. Ozawa, our dentist, thought I might need braces. I absolutely hate the idea of having braces, and I hope they find out that I don't need them. I didn't like having this extra thing to worry about this year because the regular appointments we have when school gets out are bad enough. The camp physical is even worse than the dentist. Having to pee in a jar is disgusting; and then when you have to carry the jar with your own pee in it and give it to the nurse, it is so embarrassing I would just like to die.

Sam is a doctor, and I asked him if this year he could just fill out the forms for the camp physical and check normal for everything, because I am a very healthy person. Then they could save money by having me skip going to the doctor altogether. I thought it was a great idea, but Sam said that doctors really can't do medicine on their own families. I was disappointed about this because I thought that one of the good things about Mom being married to Sam was that, because he is a doctor, I would probably never have to go to doctors again. It was real nice now, though, having Sam live with us all the time, and Sam didn't seem to be turning too much into a very clean person or yelling at my mom for stuff, and the marriage seemed to be going all right.

Sam took me to REI, which is a store that has outdoor stuff, and we bought a backpack and a new sleeping bag for camp. Sam let me pick out the sleeping bag I wanted, and he helped me try on different backpacks to see which one would be the most comfortable. I got a red sleeping bag and a red backpack to match. I was really getting excited for Happy Hollow.

When the day came to go to camp, Sam loaded my trunk into the Rabbit, and Mom and Sara and Sam and I drove to Kirkland. That's where the buses come to take everyone to camp. A lot of kids that I remembered from last year were there, and I was happy that I knew some people.

I said good-bye to Sara and hugged Mom and Sam. I was glad to be going to camp, but I felt a little sad to be leaving too. I felt that way last year too, but it's always okay once I get to Happy Hollow. Mom always cries when I leave for camp and hugs me for a long time, and this year Sam said, "I love you, Cynthia—take care of yourself." He seemed kind of sad too. I think Sara likes having Mom and Sam all to herself, but even she said she'd miss me.

When we got to Happy Hollow, we all got off the buses and went and sat on the grass around the flagpole. Mr. Sanders, the camp director, made a speech welcoming all the campers and saying stuff like how he was sure that this would be another fine season in the Happy Hollow camping tradition. Then he read the names of all the campers and told what tent we were assigned to. I was in Girls Green, which was the girls going into seventh grade. I remembered last year when I was in Girls Blue and was just going into the sixth grade. The kids in Girls Green seemed so much older because they were going to be in junior high, and now here I was being in Girls Green. I loved it.

There is a huge difference at Happy Hollow between Girls Blue and Girls Green. Our counselor seemed pretty nice too. Her name was JoAnne and she was from Bellingham, Washington, and she was going to be a junior at the University of Washington. I hoped that she wouldn't smoke pot in the bushes behind the corral and get fired. I thought I should talk that over with the kids in my tent, and maybe we could warn her about that. Mr. Sanders really checks up on everybody at Happy Hollow. I think he spends a lot of time in the bushes.

I liked the people in my tent. There were two girls from Oregon, one girl from Alaska, one girl from California, and three of us from

Seattle. I knew three people in my tent from last year, and I thought we had the best tent in the whole camp. Everything was going along perfectly, until it was time to get our pajamas on and go to bed. It was a total disaster.

I was the only one—the only person in the whole tent that didn't wear a bra. I wanted to die. It is one thing to be one of the five no-bra people in your entire sixth-grade class. But to be in Girls Green and be the only no-bra person is the most embarrassing thing in the world that could happen. I think I would really rather be a bed wetter or something like that, if I had to choose which embarrassing thing I had to have. We had a girl like that in our tent last year, her name was Bobbie Vorhees, and she was from Spokane. Right now, I would rather be Bobbie Vorhees the bed wetter from Spokane than me, Cynthia Ann Browne, the no-bra person from Seattle. It was sort of like thinking about how you would rather die—by burning to death or freezing to death.

When everyone started getting undressed, and I saw all the bras all over the place, I quickly got my pajamas and ran out of the tent to the girls' bathroom. I yelled out that I had to take a shower and no one seemed to notice. I was in such a hurry that I forgot to take my flashlight, and after I changed in the bathroom, it had gotten pretty dark. The light from the girls' bathroom lit up part of the path back to

72

the tent, but as I got farther away from the bathroom, it got darker and darker. I stayed on the path okay but it was kind of scary, and as I headed for the tent, I tripped on the root of a big tree that grew across the path. I fell flat on my face. I lay sprawled on the ground, and I could hear all the voices of the girls in Girls Green giggling away in the tent, echoing through the night. I started to cry.

I stayed there for a while, rubbing my toe which I had stubbed on the root. It really hurt, but I tried to stop crying because I didn't want anyone to find out when I got back to the tent. I finally got up and walked back slowly and carefully. When I got back to the tent, everyone was still laughing and talking, and they couldn't see that I had been crying because it was so dark.

Everyone was talking about the boys in Boys Green—those were the ones who were going into seventh grade too. Phyllis Katz from California had the bunk on top of mine, and as I crawled into my sleeping bag she asked me what I thought of one of the guys in Boys Green. I really liked Phyllis, and I knew her from last year when we had been in Girls Blue together.

"Cynthia," she said, hanging her head down upside down from the top bunk. "Did you see that cute one with the red hair and the freckles?"

I stuck my head out over the edge of my bunk and looked up at Phyllis. "Yeah, but I thought he looked too skinny." I tried to sound casual. I hoped my voice didn't sound like I had been crying.

"Maybe—but what about the blond one next to him at dinner?"

"Fine—he definitely was fine," I said, scrunching down into my sleeping bag.

Then Jane Hansen, who was one of the girls from Oregon, said that she knew him from her school and that he was from Portland too. She said his name was Chris Wheatman and he was a stuck-up creep. We all talked about Boys Green a lot more, and then finally JoAnne, our counselor, told us for the seventh time to be quiet and go to sleep. This time she sounded kind of mad, so we shut up.

Before I went to sleep, I thought a lot about what I was going to do about this bra situation. I knew I couldn't keep running to the girls' bathroom to change every time, because they would all notice for sure. I decided that the only thing I could do was to use the old gymnastics reason. I would be sure to do a bunch of cartwheels and back walkovers all over the place tomorrow and talk about how I wanted to be in the Olympics. Then when we got dressed, and I was changing into my clothes I would say, "I am so glad that I haven't grown enough to need to wear a bra like the rest of you guys, because it would sure mess up my gymnastics career." Then I would tell them that whole deal about the Russians. They might think I was weird, but I thought it would be a lot better than just standing around like a jerk while they all hooked themselves up. I still had a lump in my throat from crying, but I finally got to sleep.

The next day I did the old gymnastics thing just like I planned, and I guess they didn't think I was that weird because everyone was still pretty friendly. Especially Phyllis.

At arts and crafts in the morning we were all sitting around working on some leather stuff and were talking about our families. There weren't too many kids in my tent this year who had been divorced. Only me, Phyllis, and Gloria Appleby from Alaska. The kids who haven't been divorced seem to have trouble figuring it all out. They got confused when I told them that now that Mom and Sam are married, her last name changed to the same as Sam's last name, and Sara and my last name is the same as our real father's, and Larry and David's last name is the same as Sam's—but we all get called the wrong last names.

Some of the people at camp couldn't follow that at all, so I tried to make a chart and explain the whole thing, but it just made it more confusing, because I put Ellen in the chart next to my father, but they're not married, so they don't have the same last names either. So I just forgot about the chart. I figured as long as the people in my family know who everyone is, it doesn't matter if people at camp can't figure it out.

The kids who weren't divorced asked Phyllis and Gloria and me about what we did for the holidays. I said that at Thanksgiving our parents all try and figure out when we're going to spend the time with my mom and Sam, and when with my dad, and when Larry and David are going to be at our house, and when they're going to be with their mother. I told them about last Thanksgiving. Mom and Sam were talking about how to arrange it, and Sara wanted to just have one Thanksgiving at our house. She thought we could have it be Mom and Sam, and me, and Larry and David, and their mother, and Daddy and Ellen. Mom told her that the table wasn't big enough. But I told Phyllis that I don't think Sara had really figured out that the reason everybody got divorced in the first place was because they don't like to be together. I suppose that's because Sara loves all the people, and she wishes they would all love each other too.

"My little brother was just like that at Chanukah," Phyllis said. "He wanted my mom and my stepdad and my dad and our stepmother to all have it at our house."

Arts and crafts was almost over, and it was

time to clean up our stuff. After Phyllis said that about her little brother, I remembered the time the first Christmas after we were divorced, and my mother didn't know what to write on the Christmas cards to tell people. Sara had an idea that we should send our family picture from the year before and just cross out Daddy's face and write, "Merry Christmas, we got a divorce." But Mom didn't like that either.

After arts and crafts we had rest period; that's when we are supposed to write letters or just do what we want. Phyllis and I went back to the tent and wrote letters home. My letter was just to Mom and it went like this:

Dear Mom,

Camp is really fun this year. I like everyone in my tent and especially Phyllis Katz from California, who was here last year. The weather is fine. My counselor is nice too. I don't think she'll get fired. My favorite horse this year is a brown horse named Boots. We had chili for lunch today. There is only one terrible thing, and please don't mention this to anyone, I am the only person in all of Girls Green who doesn't wear a bra and I would like to die. Other than that everything is fine.

Love always,
Cynthia

P.S. I hate not needing a bra. Do you think I will ever grow?

I put the letter in an envelope and addressed it to Mom. I wrote just her name, Rachel Ann Lee, on the address and not Mrs. Sam Lee, because I didn't want Sam to read the letter. I also wrote "Personal—only for Mom" on the bottom of the envelope so there would be no mistake.

I kept doing cartwheels and back walkovers all over the place and talking about Nadia whatever-her-name-is, the Rumanian gymnast, who won everything and then grew and was a big loser for a while. But changing clothes before swimming and getting into our pajamas at night was still horrible. Most of the days were good at camp, but those times changing clothes in the tent never got better. I would always dread it.

Then about three days after I had sent my letter to Mom, I got a letter from her and a package at mail call. I opened the letter first. It went like this:

Dear Cynthia,

I was so happy to get your letter! I'm glad you like everyone in your tent this year. I can't wait until visiting day. I wish

Larry and David could come up with us but they'll still be at soccer camp. Uncle Dexter and Aunt Virginia are coming July 14th and we're all going salmon fishing at Westport. Sara is not so sure she wants to go. She got so seasick when we went last year.

I got a bra for you after I got your letter. Maybe your body doesn't need it right now, Cynthia, but your heart does. And that is just as important. We're just from a family of late bloomers. When I was your age I wanted a bra as badly as you do. I couldn't talk to my mother about it, so I stole one out of my big sister's drawer. It was too big so I decided to shrink it. I put it in boiling water on the stove. I figured that would do a better job than just plain hot water. I'll never forget Aunt Bonnye coming in the kitchen and seeing me there boiling her bra. It was awful!

The other night Sam and I were watching an old movie on TV. A movie star with a wonderful figure named Marilyn Monroe was in it. I told Sam I had always wished I looked like that and Sam said a very nice thing about this whole breast business. He said, "The men don't care and the boys don't count." What he meant, Cynthia, was that being a wonderful person is the most important thing about being a woman, and only boys go around valuing human beings because of what size bra they wear. But I know that since seventh-grade boys are just boys, it will still be a problem for a while.

I hope having the bra I sent will help a little bit—and at least you won't have to boil it. Have a great time at camp. I love you very much.

Mom

P.S. Sam hired Harry Z to help him clean out the gutters. Harry said to be sure and tell you hello for him.

When I had finished reading Mom's letter, I realized that I had started to cry, which really didn't make any sense to me at all because I was happy. I ran to the girls' bathroom and opened the package. It was a nice box and it said Teenform on the outside. It also said size 30AAA. I took it out of the box and put it on under my T-shirt. It seemed to fit fine, and it was really more like a kind of cut off undershirt with straps and elastic and stuff. But that was fine with me.

That afternoon when we were changing into our bathing suits for swimming, Phyllis noticed it.

"Cynthia, where did you get that?" she asked.

"Oh, my mom sent it to me today. She wrote me this letter and said I needed one. So I have to wear it. But I better not grow too much and ruin my gymnastics. That's all I need!" I said it like I was disgusted.

When I returned to the house after supper...
...and father and sister Phyllis. She said Phyllis...
...house here in Phyllis's bedroom, tomorrow and next...
...time tomorrow...
...could I would be some...

Nine

When camp was over I hated to say good-bye to Phyllis. If Phyllis lived in Seattle instead of California, I'm sure she would be my best friend instead of Trae. Phyllis Katz is just as nice as Trae Kaplan, only Phyllis is less beautiful, because she has some pimples like me. That makes for a better best friend.

Mom cried again when she met me at the bus. She always does that. She cries when I leave and she cries when I come home. My mother is a very emotional person. Sam and Sara were happy to see me too. And I was glad to be home.

It sure was good to sleep in my own bed again. Sleeping out in a tent in the woods in a sleeping bag is a very nice thing, but not forever.

Dad called after I had been home for a day and said he wanted me and Sara to come over to his apartment for dinner. Ellen was going to make the dinner. I still wished it could just be us and not her, but I was excited to see Dad, so it was okay.

When we got to Dad's apartment, Ellen was there. She usually doesn't come with Dad when he picks up Sara and me. She just waits at the apartment. I walked in and she gave me a big hug. Ellen felt my back and kind of stood back, and then she said, "Well, Cynthia, you're wearing a bra. What in the world for? You don't need one."

I have never liked Ellen, and when she said that, I wanted to absolutely murder her. How could she be so stupid! I was so embarrassed— I just wanted to go home. Dad pretended he didn't hear—thank goodness—and we all went in and sat down, while Ellen finished making the dinner.

Sara turned on the TV and we talked about camp. Talking to my father is not all that easy anymore. I don't know why, but it just isn't. It was worse today, too, because I was still so mad at Ellen, and I really didn't want to be there at all. Dad told me and Sara to go in the kitchen and see if we could help Ellen with the dinner. I didn't want to go in the kitchen or be anywhere near her, but I was afraid Dad would get mad at me if I didn't.

I went out to the kitchen and asked Ellen if she wanted any help, but she said that the dinner was ready and for all of us to come and sit down at the table.

Ellen made this casserole of gushed-up stuff, and it was horrible. It had cream of mushroom soup in it and broccoli and a bunch of other stuff that you couldn't even tell what it was. I could hardly eat it. Sara and I kept making faces at each other when she wasn't looking. The food was disgusting. Ellen also had a loaf of her special homemade bread on the table. Ellen's homemade bread is like a homemade rock. But she thinks it is wonderful, and she always makes it whenever we eat there. Then she always wraps some of it up and tells me and Sara to take it home so we can have it there. And she usually mutters something about what a shame it is that we never get homemade bread with no preservatives at our house.

When we got home from Dad's apartment, Sara and I went in the kitchen and gave the bread to Mom.

Sara went to watch TV, and as I went to the refrigerator to get something to eat, I noticed Mom putting the bread in the garbage. "I'm starving," I said. "The food was disgusting." I made myself a sandwich and sat down at the kitchen table with Mom while she had a cup of coffee.

"Know what she did this time?" I said to

Mom. "She hugged me and could tell that I had on a bra. Then she said real loud in front of Dad that I had on a bra and what in the world for and that I didn't need one."

Mom took a sip of her coffee and she looked kind of mad. "Ellen is a very insensitive person," she said quietly.

"She's a creep! You think so too—don't you, Mom?"

"A creep? Well, I guess when your father and I were first divorced I really resented Ellen. I suppose that's why I always called her 'what's-her-name-the-receptionist'—but I don't feel that way anymore."

"You mean you like her?" I was surprised.

"No, I don't like her. It would be silly to pretend I did—but it's just that resenting her got to be a big waste of time. Cynthia, being bitter doesn't feel good, and I think for the most part I've let go of it. I have to admit though that she still really gets to me when she gets you upset. But I really don't have to be involved with Ellen. It's a lot easier for me not to resent her than it is for you."

"It's hard for me to feel okay about her when I have to see her every weekend and she says mean stuff to me—and then about all Dad ever says is for me to try and understand because she's never had kids and all."

"It is harder for you," Mom said, "you're

an important part of your father's life, and she's an important part of his life too.''

"So I'm stuck with her."

"You really are, honey. I'm not sure what I can do to help you with it. I only know that if you can begin to accept her, it will be easier for you.''

"You know Ellen is so weird about you— sending us that dumb bread sort of like she's trying to act like she's better than you. Do you ever feel that way about Barbara?'' Barbara is Larry and David's mother, and I had always wondered about that, and this just seemed like a good time to ask.

"Hmmmm," Mom said, like she was thinking. "I guess I do in a way—feel a little weird about her, although I don't think it's the same kind of weird that Ellen feels about me."

"Well, what kind of weird is it?''

"It's hard to explain, but I guess that it's not that I'm afraid Sam would ever want to get back together with Barbara. I know he loves me, and that if they had been able to get along and work out their marriage, they would have long before Sam met me. So I'm not worried about that. It's more like just wishing sometimes that Sam and I were the mother and the father of the same children. Barbara is the mother of Sam's two children, and that is something that I'm never going to be."

"Is that why your voice sounds so funny

whenever you answer the phone and it's Barbara?"

"Does my voice really sound funny when Barbara calls?"

"Yeah—real strange."

Mom laughed. "Well, I guess it's pretty hard for me to hide that I'm not all that comfortable talking to her."

"Why is that?"

"I guess wives and ex-wives can never really be comfortable with each other."

"Kind of like dogs and cats?"

"Exactly," Mom smiled. Then she told me that I had better get ready for bed and that it was getting late.

I thought since I'm going to be in the seventh grade that I should be able to go to bed later than I did last year. Mom said that she'd talk to Sam about it. She always has to talk everything over with Sam.

The next day Larry and David came over. I hadn't seen them since before I went to camp, and it wasn't so bad being with them at first. Although I did wish that I could have had a little more time with Mom and Sam without them there. After all, I'd been away at camp for a long time, and it seemed to me I deserved more time at home without being invaded so soon by them.

They had a great time at the Seattle Sounders' Soccer Camp, only now Larry acted like he was a better soccer player than me, and it kind of made me mad. Larry's hero on the Seattle Sounders was Tony Chursky, who used to be the goalie until he got traded. Larry read in the paper that Tony Chursky takes ballet lessons so that he can learn how to leap real high. That is supposed to help him leap in the air to catch the balls when he is being the goalie, and now Larry is going to take ballet lessons too. I think it is ridiculous.

Now there are four soccer players in our family, because Sam is going to be on a team too. He's going to be on the Mount Baker neighborhood men's team, which is called the Seattle Flounders. The men on the team are all old. They are at least forty, and I don't think they know how to play soccer very well. I think that's why they are called the Flounders. Sam wanted to practice up for the Flounders, so on Sunday, Sam, Larry, David, and I went down to the park with the soccer ball. Sam seemed to pay the most attention to Larry, and he was trying to get Larry to show him some of the stuff that he had learned at the Seattle Sounders' Soccer Camp. Here I am, the star striker of the Roto Rooters, and just because I went to Happy Hollow instead of the Seattle Sounders' dumb soccer camp, I got practically ignored. I was really mad, so I just left the park and walked back up to the house. I don't even think Sam knew I was gone.

When I got home I went in the kitchen and decided to fix myself a big bowl of ice cream. I opened the freezer door and took out the ice cream carton. I opened the carton and stuck the spoon in. It was empty.

"Those creeps!" I yelled. "Mom, they ate all the ice cream!"

Mom came into the kitchen and told me to calm down, and that the food around here is for everyone, and said I should eat fruit.

"I do not want to eat fruit. I want to eat ice cream!"

"Cynthia, I am not going to buy a separate carton of ice cream for you and Sara and for Larry and David. That's ridiculous—you kids are just going to have to learn to share."

"I think putting an empty carton of ice cream back in the freezer is really low."

"Cynthia, I do not want to talk about this. Eat a banana if you want a snack."

"I do not want to eat a banana."

"Well, I'm not going to discuss this anymore," she said, walking out of the kitchen.

I was making myself a peanut butter and jelly sandwich when Sam and Larry and David came back from the park. Larry and David were dribbling the soccer ball around in the house, but Mom didn't say a word to them about it. She never lets me do that, and I have been mad about this for a long time, and I'm especially mad about it now.

"Here's the ballet star," I said to Larry, and I leaped around the kitchen.

"Shut up, Cynthia. Tony Chursky is a great goalie and he takes ballet."

"Yeah, well, if he's so great, how come we lost to the Cosmos and it was all his stupid fault!"

"It was not!"

"It was too!"

"It was not! You don't know anything about it. Mickey Cave scored a goal in that game and the referee said we were off sides and we weren't!"

"So what—it was still Chursky's fault. He should practice soccer instead of ballet. I'm glad he got traded. Not even the Roto Rooters take ballet, and we're a girls' team."

"Roto Rooters! What a crappy name. Ha ha ha."

I was having enough of this dumb argument with Larry, and I went upstairs to call Trae. On the way upstairs I heard Mom and Sam talking in the living room, and it sounded like they were fighting too. Sam had come in kind of limping after playing soccer, and Mom was telling him he should be careful, that he wasn't as young as he used to be, and that forty-year-old men just couldn't move around the same way they could when they were twenty. Sam was sounding kind of mad and said for Mom not to bug him about it, that he was going to play on the Flounders, and that was all there was to it.

I called Trae, but she wasn't home. I even called Helene, but she wasn't home either. So I decided to walk down to Harry's. I just had to get out of the house. I guess I was pretty desperate to want to go down to Harry Z's, but I really couldn't stand being home. Mom and Sam were still arguing about the Flounders when I left.

Harry was out in his yard raking leaves. "Hi, Cynthia. Where are you going?" Harry asked.

"Oh, nowhere special—just walking around. Things are kind of boring today . . . there's not much to do." I didn't want Harry Z to think that I had meant to walk down to his house.

"Want to help me rake leaves? I'll make you a deal—"

"Harry, I do not want to make any deals, and I do not want to rake leaves. Actually I'm in a rotten mood."

"So what else is new?" Harry said and laughed.

"I'm not always in a rotten mood!"

"Yeah, I know—well, what's wrong anyway?"

"Oh, I just had a fight with Larry, and now Mom and Sam are fighting about the Flounders."

"Oh yeah, the men's soccer team. Mr. Leadbetter next door is on that. He's been out practicing in his yard a lot. He puffs around and falls down quite a bit. I ought to give him some lessons—I'll bet he'd go for it if the price was right.''

''Mr. Leadbetter would never pay you to give him soccer lessons—that's ridiculous!''

''You never know—he might go for it,'' Harry said, raking up a big pile of leaves. ''Well, what's wrong with your mom and Sam? Do you think they're going to get a divorce?''

''Of course not! They're just fighting about the Flounders—it's no big deal.''

''I don't know, Cynthia,'' Harry said, taking off his glasses and waving them around, ''that's sometimes just how these things start.''

''Thanks a lot, Harry,'' I said disgustedly. ''Thanks just a whole big bunch,'' and I stomped off down the street.

What a creep! I didn't want him to see how upset I was. But what if Harry was right? What if Mom and Sam were going to get a divorce? I hated it when Daddy left, and now to think that Sam could leave too . . . it was just awful. I started to cry. Damn that Harry! I kicked the leaves along the sidewalk. I don't know what I'd do if Sam left. Having another father leave me would hurt so awful I don't think I could stand it. The whole idea was horrible, and it made me practically sick inside just to think about it.

When I got home things were pretty quiet.

Mom was down in the basement working on her pottery, and Sam was in the living room reading. Larry, David, and Sara were watching TV. I went up to my room and closed the door. I got out my diary and started a new page. It went like this:

THINGS I HATE TODAY

1. *Harry Zimmerman*
2. *STEPBROTHERS*

Then I made another page.

THINGS I AM WORRIED ABOUT

1. *Mom and Sam getting divorced.*

Then I closed the diary, locked it with the little key, and put it back in the box marked "Old Underwear for Goodwill," where I kept the Ding-Dongs that I had stashed away so they wouldn't get eaten up by THEM!

Ten

Helene called. She wanted to know if Larry was at our house.

"Yeah, he's here, but they're leaving pretty soon."

"Why do they have to leave?" she asked.

"Because Helene, they don't live here all the time—they live with Barbara, their mother, and they have to go soon because everyone has to get ready for school tomorrow." Actually I lied. Larry and David weren't leaving until tonight, but I just couldn't stand the idea of Helene coming over and chasing Larry all over the place like I knew she wanted to.

"Oh well, are you all ready for school tomorrow—what are you wearing?"

"I haven't really thought about it, Helene." That was a lie too, because Trae and I had been on the phone every day since I got back from camp discussing the different outfits we might wear, and also trying on a bunch of stuff.

"I guess I'm going to wear my overalls."

"That's nice, Helene—well bye." I hung up the phone.

Trae and I had narrowed down our outfits to two. She was either going to wear a brown blazer and a tweed skirt, or her gray pants and a matching gray cowl-neck sweater. People are starting to wear skirts and dresses a lot more this year. It's different from the sixth grade, when Rosemary Babcock was the only one.

I hadn't decided whether I'd wear my gray and pink plaid skirt with a pink vest sweater that went over this silky blouse that has real big sleeves, or if I'd wear my plaid blouse with a gold chain that has the letter "C" for Cynthia on it, with my Brittania jeans with the scroll pocket. It was a very big decision. Trae and I finally decided to stick with pants for the first day. Then, if there were enough people wearing skirts, we'd probably wear them on the second day. We hadn't figured our clothes out for the whole rest of the week yet. But we didn't think that would be a good idea, because it was important to see what everyone else had on—especially the eighth and ninth graders.

After I finished talking to Helene I went downstairs and everyone was watching the Seahawks on TV. Our family is crazy about the

Sounders first, the Seahawks and the Sonics are tied for second, and we don't care about the Mariners. That's the baseball team. I like to watch the Seahawks a lot. Although I don't always entirely understand football, I do get the main idea of what it's all about, and mostly for me, what it's all about is Jim Zorn. I am in love with Jim Zorn. He is the best looking football player. He is the quarterback and he is the star. You never know if he is going to pass or run or what. Sometimes or what is getting sacked a lot, but that's okay because he is very flashy to watch. One of the sad things of my life is that I think I am too young for Jim Zorn. He is in his twenties, and twelve is just too young for that. Maybe it will help when I turn thirteen.

Sara only likes to watch the Seahawks when they show the person jumping around in the Seahawk costume. They were showing the game more than the bird, so Sara left and went up to her room to play with her Barbie stuff.

She was only gone a minute when she came running back downstairs and started yelling that David had gotten in her room and wrecked all her stuff. Sara was really mad! Mom didn't say anything, she just kept watching the game, and then sort of acted like she didn't know what to do about it. If I had been the one who had wrecked Sara's Barbie stuff, there is no question that she would know what to do about it.

I would get it for sure. But Mom just kept watching the game. Sara kept yelling about it.

Sam went over to the TV and turned the sound down a little. "Sara, I know you're upset that David got in your stuff, and you have a right to be. We need to talk about this kind of thing, and if you can wait until halftime, which is in just a few minutes, we'll all talk about it." Then he held out his arms to Sara, and she went over to him and sat in his lap, and we watched the end of the second quarter until it was halftime. She was happier because they showed the Seahawk bird jumping around a little bit.

At halftime Sam turned off the TV and said that it seemed like everyone was getting on each other's nerves around here lately, and he wondered if anyone had any ideas about what we could do about it.

"If David would just stay out of my stuff, everything would be fine!" Sara said.

"Yeah," I said. "And I get sick of all the ice cream getting eaten up and there's none for me. But the worst thing is, how come Mom lets Larry and David do a whole bunch of stuff that Sara and I can't—like playing soccer in the house and stuff like that?"

"Cynthia," Mom said, "I am trying to be a good stepmother. Every single fairy tale had a wicked stepmother in it, and it's as if stepmothers are the most terrible people of all, and I don't want to be like that."

Sam turned to me and said, "You know, we really are trying our best to help everyone get along in this family. It's hard to always think about the feelings of four children instead of just two."

I said, "Well, so what if Cinderella's stepmother was a creep, and Snow White's stepmother was a rotten person, and Hansel and Gretel's stepmother sent them out in the woods to starve? I don't see why that has anything to do with Larry and David drinking Coke in the living room, getting in Sara's stuff, playing soccer in the house, and eating anything they want, when Sara and I have to ask—ESPECIALLY EATING ALL THE DING-DONGS when me and Sara can't!"

No one said anything for a while, and then Larry said that he wished I'd get off his case about Chursky, and for me to quit saying all that stuff about ballet.

David looked up from the table where he had been drawing a little picture of a car. "I think there should be the same rules for everybody. Sometimes I wish I could live here all the time so it would be more like my house and not like I'm a visitor because I don't like Sara and Cynthia to be mad at me."

Mom went over and hugged David because he had started to cry. Then, for no reason, Sara cried and I cried and Larry cried and even Mom and Sam. It was ridiculous, our whole family was sitting around sniffling.

Then Sara got off Sam's lap and stood up and said, "We need a dog."

Everyone laughed at first, but then David said he wanted a dog too. Larry said, "Yeah, that's not a bad idea—we could all go pick it out and it could belong to all of us."

"Great idea! Let's get a dog today!" I said. I had always wanted a dog, ever since a dog we had a long time ago got hit by a car. I really did want a new dog, and I figured Martha could learn how to get along with it, especially if we got a little puppy.

Even Mom seemed excited. "What do you think, Sam?"

Sam smiled. "It's okay with me, but the kids will have to do all the work feeding it and taking care of it. Cynthia and Sara will have to do it during the week, and Larry and David will have to do their share on the weekends. I don't want any part of cleaning up after a dog."

We said we would do all the work, and then we bugged Mom and Sam a whole lot to take us to the dog pound today to get the dog. We always get dogs at the pound because Mom believes that if you ever have dogs or cats you should get the kind that you save from the pound. At the dog pound, if they don't get homes for the dogs after a few days, they put them to sleep, which is just a polite way of saying that they get killed.

Sam said we could go after the Seahawks game was over, and we were really excited. Larry and I stayed with Mom and Sam to watch the game, but David and Sara went up to Sara's room to look in this animal book she had that had a lot of pictures of dogs. They were excited about figuring out what kind of a dog they wanted to get.

The Seahawks won the game, which was great, because they beat the Oakland Raiders and we all hate the Oakland Raiders. They are a very mean team. It was a wonderful score. I think it ended up 28 for the Seahawks and 7 for the crummy Raiders. Sam yelled and Mom and Larry and I did too. Jim Zorn was especially wonderful that day.

After the game was over, we all got in the Rabbit and headed for the pound. Sam let me roll down the sunroof because it was a beautiful day. I was so happy—that is, until we got to the dog pound.

I think that the dog pound is just about the saddest place in the whole world. All the dogs are in these cages, and it smells bad and you walk down the rows looking at them. They all bark or cry and then come up to the wire and try and look adorable so you will adopt them. I would like to adopt every dog in the whole place. They also have these signs over the cages that tell you how long the dogs have been there. One sign says "First Day," and there are a bunch of dogs in cages under that sign. Then there is a sign that says "Second Day," with the dogs under that. The worst sign of all says "Third Day," and all the dogs in the cages under that sign are the most pitiful, because it means that unless they get adopted that day, the next day they will be put to sleep—which is killed. You only have one day to save those dogs' lives. I hate the dog pound.

We were all mostly looking at the dogs that were under the sign that said "Third Day." Sara and David ran up to the cage where they had the ugliest dog I have ever seen. It was a tiny, puny little thing that looked more like a brown rat than a dog. While they were looking at that little dog, Larry and I found a gorgeous puppy, which was also under the third-day sign. The sign on the cage said that it was a female and that it was half Lab and half Shepherd. I looked at Larry and he looked at me.

"That's the one," he said, smiling.

"The perfect dog," I agreed.

We went back to tell Mom and Sam that we had found the right dog. But Sara and David were talking to them and jumping all around because they wanted to adopt that little shrimpy dog that looked like a rat. I couldn't believe that anyone would want such a pitiful excuse for a dog.

We told Mom and Sam to come and look at our dog. We were sure the minute they saw her they would know that it was the perfect dog for our family. Sam and Mom agreed that it seemed like a nice dog, but then David and Sara made them come and look at their stupid dog. They begged them to get it. David and Sara both kept jumping up and down, saying they just had to have it. They said "please" about a million times.

"You don't really want that rat!" Larry said, looking at the dog they wanted. "The dogs next door might eat it for dinner," and Larry and I both laughed.

Mom looked at Sam. "What are we going to do?"

"Just have two dogs," Sara said. "They can be friends."

"Yeah, if our dog doesn't eat yours for lunch!" Larry said, laughing.

Then Sara started to cry. "Mom, no one in the whole world would want this poor little dog. If we don't get it—it will die . . . tomorrow!"

Mom looked at Sam again. "What do you think, Sam? Maybe two dogs really aren't that much more trouble than one—"

Sam didn't seem convinced, but he looked at Sara and David sticking their hands through the cage and petting the little dog, and then he looked at me and Larry standing by the cage admiring our dog. "Okay," he said, "but Sara is entirely responsible for cleaning up after that dog during the week, and David has to take care of it on the weekends. And the same thing goes for you two big shots—" he said, turning to me and Larry. "Cynthia, you have to take care of it during the week, and Larry on the weekends."

We all agreed and promised and crossed our hearts and all that stuff that we would and that Sam would never even be bothered by the dogs. Then Mom filled out the papers and paid five dollars for each dog, and we got in the car.

Sara and David sat next to each other with their little rat on their laps, and Larry and I took turns holding our puppy. She had giant feet, and we knew she would grow up to be a big important dog.

Mom turned around to the back seat where we were sitting holding the dogs. "What are you going to name them?" she asked.

We thought of names all the way home, but couldn't agree on anything. Finally Larry looked at the little puny one that Sara and David were holding and then he looked at our wonderful big puppy.

"I've got it—Laverne and Shirley."

And so we named the dogs Laverne and Shirley. And we were all sure that there would never be any problems.

Eleven

I had all my clothes picked out for the first day of seventh grade. Only there were two things I hadn't planned on. The seventh grade never started. At least it didn't start on the day it was supposed to because there was a school strike. The teachers wanted more money, so they didn't go to work. During that week I had to go to the orthodontist on Mercer Island. His name is Dr. Turner. Mom really likes Dr. Turner, so we have to drive across the dumb bridge just for me to go there. And I had to get braces. So when the seventh grade finally did start, there I was in the outfit I had planned— my plaid blouse and my Brittania jeans with the scroll pocket and my gold chain with my initial on it. But the part of the outfit I had not planned on was my braces. Yuk.

But the seventh grade was really exciting. The school seemed absolutely huge, and Trae and I and all the other kids from our sixth-grade class had to take a bus to get there. I was taking language arts, math, woodshop, physical education, Spanish, and communications. I had three men teachers, which I am not used to because in elementary school there aren't that many men teachers. I hope I get my period sometime soon, but I sure hope I don't get it in Spanish, math or woodshop, because those teachers are all men, and I would just die.

But the most wonderful thing about the whole seventh grade was the person whose locker was right next to mine—Seth Rosen. Seth Rosen has the longest eyelashes I have ever seen on a boy, and he is taller than me, and that is especially important because most of the boys in the seventh grade seem to be shorter than me. And he has nice shoulders and always wears nice stuff.

Seth Rosen is the most wonderful boy I had ever seen in my life. He didn't go to the same elementary school with me. He came to our junior high from the North End, because we have busing and he is getting bused. I think busing is wonderful, because if there were no busing, Seth Rosen would not be at Martin Luther King Junior High.

Trae and I talked about school all the way home on the bus. We didn't have any classes together, which I was sad about. But we did have the same lunch period—which is the most important thing anyway. Trae is now definitely in love with Richie Hinkley and that doesn't bother me that much anymore now that I have seen Seth Rosen. Richie has math with me, and Trae wants me to ask him what he thinks of her. I asked Trae if she had Seth Rosen in any of her classes, but she doesn't know who he is yet. I'm going to point him out to her tomorrow.

Trae thinks that if I want Seth Rosen to know who I am that I should drop all my books right in front of him while I'm going to my locker. Then I could pick them up and say I was sorry and talk to him. I think it's a pretty good idea. We also discussed the possibility of pretending that my locker was stuck and then for me to ask him to come over and help me un-stuck it. I kind of like that plan better. I'm not sure that dropping your books on someone's foot is that charming.

Trae is going to wear her skirt tomorrow, and she's been shaving her legs. We also talked a lot about that on the way home, and I'm not so sure if I want to do it. I suppose I'll decide on the day we have PE when I find out how many other people are shaving their legs. I sure am glad we only have PE with the girls in the seventh grade. I absolutely couldn't believe how big some of those ninth graders are. We all look like midgets compared to them—not

106

started yelling at him that he was too old to be on the Flounders and that's why he got hurt. And then Sam yelled that being on the Flounders had nothing to do with dog poo. It was awful. They were so mad, and then finally Sam just got up and limped up to the shower and slammed the door so hard I thought the whole house would fall down.

Larry and I cleaned up the dog poo because we could tell it was Laverne's because she is so much bigger than Shirley—so her dog poo is bigger. I hate cleaning up dog poo. After we got it all cleaned up, the phone rang. It was Helene.

"Hi, Cynthia, is Larry there?"

"Yes—he's here."

"Wonderful—I'll be right over. Bye."

Helene hung up before I had a chance to say anything. She makes me so mad. I really can't stand her coming over here and making such a big deal about Larry. She acts like I'm not even here.

As soon as I got off the phone with Helene, the phone rang again. I picked it up and there was no one there. Just a lot of breathing.

"Hello . . ." I said.

There was silence, just some breathing and then some giggling.

"Hello, who is this?"

More breathing and giggling.

"Well, if you're not going to talk, whoever-you-are, I'm hanging up," and I slammed down the phone.

Then Helene came and went right over to Larry like I wasn't even there. She hardly spoke to me at all. This was getting to be too much. Helene hardly speaks to me and some-one calls up and just breathes. I went up to my room. While I was in my room, the phone rang again. I ran to my mom's room and answered it.

"Hello."

Silence, only this time there was more gig-gling but also breathing.

"Listen, whoever-you-are, this isn't funny. Good-bye," and I slammed the phone down again.

I could hear Larry and Helene laughing and joking around downstairs, and it just made me madder. The only person paying attention to me was the breather, and I didn't even know who it was. I went back in my room and slammed the door.

I got my diary out from the box marked "Old Underwear for Goodwill" and turned to a clean page. Across the page I saw the last stuff I had written where it said, *"THINGS I WORRY ABOUT,"* and then it said *1. Mom and Sam getting divorced.* I just stared at the page and then I started crying. The fight they had when Sam fell in Laverne's dog poo was just awful. Maybe Harry was right and that was how it started. Maybe they really were going to get a divorce. I guess I was crying a lot louder than I thought because Mom must have heard me. She came to my room and knocked on the door.

"Cynthia, are you all right? Can I come in?"

I got up from my bed and let her in. Then I sat back down on my bed. Mom sat next to me and put her arms around me.

"Something is really bothering you, Cynthia—what is it?"

It was hard to talk. I had been crying so much. Mom sat with me and rubbed my back. She glanced down at my diary and saw the page where I had written that I was worried about Mom and Sam getting a divorce.

"Oh, so that's it! You're afraid that Sam and I will get a divorce?"

I nodded. I had been crying too much to be able to talk.

Mom hugged me for a long time. I got big tear blobs on her blouse. "Cynthia," she said, "love is like a little plant. People need to take care of it so it can stay healthy—just like plants."

"Like plants?"

"Sure. Plants need to have water, fresh air, sunshine, and have weeds and bugs taken away. Love is just like that."

"What do weeds and bugs have to do with love?" Sometimes Mom says stuff that doesn't always make sense to me.

"Well, when people love each other and take good care of the love, it can stand up under all the bad times. It's like a plant that's had good care so it can last through the bad times."

"Like when it gets cold and when there's not enough water and stuff like that?" I asked.

"Exactly like that—and just like there are always bad times like that for plants, there are for people too."

"So I shouldn't worry about Sam being mad because he fell in Laverne's dog poo?"

Mom laughed. "Well, remember to clean up the dog poo—but don't worry about me and Sam. I love Sam and Sam loves me and you and all of us, and it will be all right. It's good that Sam and I can fight."

"How can that be good! I hate it when you fight! All I can think about is that you'll get another divorce and that Sam will leave." My throat got this lump in it again.

Mom hugged me some more. "Cynthia, it's good that we can fight because, well—it means we have faith that we love each other. That's all, and we know getting mad won't destroy it. People who love you don't stop loving you just because sometimes you get mad at them."

"But didn't that happen with you and Daddy?"

"Yes it did—the fights and getting mad did eventually destroy it, but the difference is that Daddy and I didn't take good care of how we loved each other. And we also married so young and really changed over the years. But the way we had loved each other, well, we just took it for granted—like it was a little plant that didn't need anything, and we forgot to water it and put it in the sunshine. So when the bad times came, it just couldn't take it."

"Are you sure you and Sam know how to take care of it?" I wiped my eyes.

Mom smiled. "Well, maybe because this is a second marriage for Sam and me, it makes us like the Avis Rent A Car company. We're number two so we try harder!"

That made me laugh. Mom hugged me again, and we both laughed some more about the Avis car company marriage.

As she started to leave, I said, "Mom—one more thing. Could you tell me again how you and Sam try harder. You know, exactly what do you do to make it real strong and take good care of it?"

"Well, I guess kind of like what you and I did just now—we just keep talking things over and trying hard to understand how the other person feels."

"Mom, you take good care of all the plants around here." Mom laughed, but her eyes seemed shiny. I think she had maybe been crying too. As I said before, my mother is a very emotional person.

I put my diary back in the box in my closet. Then the phone rang again. This time the voice said, "Cynthia?" when I answered it. But then there was just a bunch of giggling and more breathing. I wondered who it was.

Twelve

The seventh grade was going to have a roller-skating party. I was so excited I could hardly stand it. Trae and I had been talking on the phone all week trying to figure out what we would wear. Besides being excited for the party, I was also very scared. I mean, what if no one asked me to skate with them?

It would be awful, and I love to roller-skate too. I am one of the best roller-skaters in the entire seventh grade at Martin Luther King— I am just sure of that. At least I could count on Harry Z. I mean, I know at least I could skate with Harry Z, if no one else asked me to skate on the couples' skate. But still I was pretty worried about the whole thing.

Things seemed okay with Mom and Sam. The other night while they were making dinner I heard them laugh a lot, and then I went in the kitchen and saw them kissing while Mom was stirring the beans.

The breather called four times this week. Sometimes when Mom or Sam answers the phone, the breather just hangs up. But whenever I answer he says, "Cynthia-uh-uh—" then he just breathes and giggles. The breather is definitely driving me crazy.

It seemed like it would be about four hundred years until the day of the roller-skating party. But the day finally came. Sam drove us there, and Trae's mother, Mrs. Kaplan, was going to pick us up. The party was at Skate-King over in Bellevue, and Martin Luther King Junior High had reserved the whole place just for the seventh graders from our school. Trae wore her navy blue pants with her white blouse and her baby blue sweater. I finally decided on my red turtle neck and the same Brittania scroll-pocket jeans I had worn the first day of school.

There were seven of us in the car. Me and Trae and Olvita Johnson, Rosemary Babcock, Helene (who wormed her way into it, even though she doesn't go to our school—just because Mom is such good friends with her mother), Shelly Mahoney, and Rosetta Jackson. Those are all my favorite people in the entire seventh grade (except, of course, for Helene, who wouldn't be my favorite, even if she did go to Martin Luther King Junior High).

Sam dropped us all off at Skate-King, and we went in and rented our skates. The music was terrific. There was a long line to get skates, but Trae and I finally got them, and the pair I ended up with wasn't too bad.

We went into the bathroom before we started skating—just to comb our hair and stuff like that.

Trae had put on some lip gloss and handed some to me. "Here, Cynthia, put some of this on—it really looks good."

I took the cap off and carefully touched the lip gloss to my mouth. It did look good. Trae was right.

We combed our hair some more and then headed out to the rink. Everyone, absolutely everyone, was there. The first boy from our class that I looked for, of course, was Seth Rosen. He was skating around with Richie and a bunch of guys I didn't know. Trae and I started skating and it was really fun. Seth and Richie caught up with us and started skating next to us making faces and trying to do shoot the duck.

"That's Seth Rosen next to Richie—what do you think?" I asked Trae.

Trae was kind of wobbling along, and she would grab my arm every once in a while because she can't skate very well. She turned around to see Seth, but then she fell down.

"You weren't supposed to make it so obvious," I said, laughing, as I helped her up.

"He's really a fox, Cynthia. Did you see Richie?"

"Yeah—he's over in the far corner sort of chasing Harry Z around."

The free skate was almost over and they said the next skate would be a couples' skate. I started to sweat. I was so nervous. What if no one asked me? I would just die. Maybe I could pretend I had gotten sick and just hide out in the girls' bathroom for the rest of the party. Although I really didn't want to do that because I love roller-skating.

"EVERYONE OFF THE RINK," the announcer yelled. "FREE SKATE IS OVER. THE NEXT SKATE WILL BE FOR COUPLES ONLY."

We all got off the rink and lined up against the edge. Trae was one of the first ones to get picked. Richie Hinkley came right over to her.

"Wanna skate?" he asked casually.

Trae smiled. "Sure, Richie," and then he took her hand and they went out on the rink. Now I was all alone. I couldn't stand this waiting. Rosemary Babcock was not far away from me, and these guys were all asking her to skate. Hugh Normanski, Bill Coach, and of all people, Harry Z was hanging around her drooling all over the place. Now I was really worried. Harry Z, at least, I thought would come through for me if no one else did, and now here he was drooling all over Rosemary Babcock. I thought maybe it was a good time for me to get sick and just go the girls' bathroom. I was sure no one would ever ask me. It seemed like I had been standing there for a million hours, when someone tapped me on the shoulder.

"Cynthia," he said, "wanna skate?"

I turned around and it was Seth Rosen. I couldn't believe it. I was so happy I didn't know what to say. I just stood there frozen like a dummy.

"Well, if you don't want to—that's okay," he said and started to turn away.

"No, wait, I'd love to," I said, smiling.

Seth took my hand, which had so much sweat on it I thought he would just say "yuk" and drop it, but he didn't, and we went out on the rink.

Seth and I skated around, and he was a wonderful skater. He even turned in front of me and skated backwards while he was holding both my hands. Then he said, "Now you try it."

I turned around and skated backwards, holding both his hands, and we were gliding around, it was heaven . . . only when I tried to turn to get back to be skating next to him, Harry Z was coming up alongside of me, skating with Rosemary Babcock, and Harry stuck out his foot and I tripped. I fell right down, and then Seth fell too. I was so embarrassed. But Seth got right up and held out his hand and helped me up, and he had his arm around my shoulder too.

"Don't worry about Harry," he said, "the guy's a weirdo."

"I know," I said as we skated around. "I've lived on the same block with him my whole life."

Trae and Richie skated by, and they were falling all over the place because Richie kept having to hold Trae up.

We waved to them. "You're a great skater," Seth said to me while we went gliding by Trae and Richie.

"Thanks—so are you," I said with a big smile.

"Hey, you have braces," he said, looking at me. "I never noticed before."

I was so embarrassed that Seth had noticed my braces. So I just closed my mouth real tight.

Then he said, "So do I—I go to Dr. Turner on Mercer Island. Who do you go to?"

I couldn't believe it. I had never noticed that Seth Rosen had braces, and now to find out that he went to the very same orthodontist, well—I just couldn't believe it!

"You're kidding," I said, "I go to Dr. Turner too." The couples' skate was over and it was time for a free skate, but Seth didn't leave. He just stayed with me and we kept skating around holding hands. The whole thing was like a dream come true.

"How d'ya like it when they put all that plaster junk in your mouth to take impressions of your teeth?" he asked.

"It was awful! I thought I would die!"

"Me too," Seth said, "I started to gag and everything." Then Seth pretended he was choking, and he let go of my hand and did imitations of a person choking on the plaster stuff. It was real funny and I laughed a lot.

He skated back over to me and we held hands again. Rosemary Babcock skated by and she was being followed by a whole pack of guys from our class. Not only Harry Z, but Hugh Normanski, Bill Coach, and Josh Gibbs. Rosemary is about ten feet taller than all of them, and it looked silly.

The next skate was a couples' skate again, and Seth and I just kept skating. The song they played was "Always and Forever," and they made the lights kind of dark while all these other lights would flash around the ring sparkling like diamonds. Seth let go of my hand and slipped his arm around my waist and I put my arm around his waist. Trae and Richie skated by again, and they were still falling all over the place. Seth and I laughed.

"You're really good at sports," he said. "From my math class third period I can watch your PE class playing soccer out on the field."

"Really? I didn't know anyone could see us."

"Well, I can, and you're the best player out there. I like girls who are good at sports. Wanna try skating backwards again?"

"Okay." Seth skated forwards and I turned around him and skated backwards only this time instead of holding hands he put his arms around my waist and I put my arms around his neck. There didn't seem to be anywhere else to put them. It was wonderful.

"I sure like your braces," he said, laughing.

"I like yours too!" Then he took my arm and pulled me around next to him and we skated forwards next to each other with our arms around each other's waists. They were still playing "Always and Forever" and the lights were still sparkling like diamonds all over the rink.

"Cynthia," Seth said in a kind of funny voice. "I know this sounds kind of stupid—but I've been trying to call you up for a long time. Richie Hinkley is always over at my house when I call, and he just gets me laughing and then I hang up."

"You mean you're the breather!" I said. I was so surprised.

"The what?"

"Well, it's just that I never could figure out who it was that was calling up, because they would just laugh and then I could hear them breathing—so I just thought of that person as the breather.''

''Yeah . . . I guess that's me, but what I was wondering, Cynthia, is—uh if uh—well. I was wondering if you'd come and watch my next soccer game? And then maybe I could come and watch one of yours?''

I was so happy I didn't know what to do or say. So I just put my head on his shoulder while we skated around to ''Always and Forever,'' and I just whispered ''Uh-huh'' real close to him, because that seemed like the best thing to do at the time.

At ten o'clock they turned all the lights on real bright and the seventh grade roller-skating party was over. Seth and I said good-bye, and he said he'd see me Monday at school.

When Mrs. Kaplan dropped me off at home, I practically floated into the house. Mom and Sam were waiting up, and I kissed them both good night and danced up the stairs humming ''Always and Forever.'' When I got ready for bed I brushed my teeth, but I didn't wash my hands because Seth had been holding them and I didn't want to wash them ever again. I got into bed and my heart was pounding. It was the most wonderful night of my whole life. Right before I went to sleep I got up and got my diary out of the box. I made a new page.

THINGS I LOVE

1. *Seth Rosen*
2. *roller-skating*
3. *"Always and Forever"*
4. *Seth Rosen*

Then I locked it up with the key and put it in the box and went to sleep.

The next day was Sunday and I slept pretty late. When I went downstairs, Mom and Sam and Larry and David and Sara were all eating pancakes.

Mom asked if I had a good time at the party, and I said that it was okay. Then we all went in the living room and Sam turned on the football game, and we just sat around and watched football and read the funnies from the Sunday paper.

Sam couldn't stay too long, though, because he was on call at the hospital and had to get over there and check on some patients.

There was some kind of a quiz that Sara was trying to fill out that was in the Things-for-Children-to-Do section of the Sunday paper. She sat there trying to figure it out and finally she asked David about one of the questions. I guess she was stuck.

"David, this question says, 'Old MacDonald Had a ———,' and I don't know what to put in the blank."

"Farm, dummy," David said, while he was looking at Snoopy in the funnies.

"Oh, of course—farm," Sara said, turning back to the quiz. Then she looked up at David again.

"How do you spell 'farm,' David?"

"That's easy," David said. "Farm is spelled e-i-e-i-o." Larry and I laughed so hard we could hardly stand it.

"Farm is spelled 'e-i-e-i'—ha-ha-ha-ha-ha."

Then David got mad and threw a pillow at Larry, and Larry threw one back, and pretty soon we were all throwing the pillows from the couches and the chairs all over the place. It was great!

But Mom didn't think it was great at all. She came running back into the living room from the kitchen and started screaming at all of us to cut it out and to clean up all the mess. She was furious. Not just at me and Sara—but she was furious at Larry and David too—she gave equal time to everybody about being furious and told us to knock it off and clean it all right up—or else.

Sara said, "But Mom, we're just having fun, like the Brady Bunch." That was definitely the wrong thing to say because Mom got even madder.

"YOU ARE NOT THE BRADY BUNCH—AND I AM NOT MRS. BRADY BECAUSE MRS. BRADY HAS ALICE WHO DOES

ALL THE WORK SO MRS. BRADY CAN GO AROUND LOOKING ADORABLE ALL THE TIME AND WE DON'T HAVE AN AL-ICE! We just have me and Mrs. Swenson, who only comes a half-a-day once every two weeks, and YOU ARE GOING TO CLEAN UP ALL THIS MESS!''

My mother was not sounding at all like she was afraid to be the wicked stepmother like in all the fairy tales. She was mad at me and mad at Larry and mad at Sara and mad at David— she was mad at all of us.

Larry and I did almost all the work, and Sara and David just fooled around taking about ten hours just to pick up one feather. One of the couch pillows had come apart and there were feathers all over the place. They made us so mad that we got away from them and went up to my room, and Larry practiced karate and I practiced gymnastics.

Up in my room I stood on my head and put my feet up against the wall. Larry was practicing doing karate kicks in the air. We also took Laverne up there with us.

"Larry," I said, "you know, sometimes I get sick of being the oldest."

"So do I—David gets away with everything, and I always get blamed just 'cause I'm older."

"That's how it is with me and Sara." I got tired of standing on my head and talking upside down. I went and sat on my bed.

"Do you want some Ding-Dongs?" I asked.

"We don't have any, do we?"

"Well—not that anybody knows about—but if you promise not to tell David or Sara—I'll show you."

"Sure I promise," Larry said, smiling.

Larry followed me in my closet and watched while I took the Ding-Dongs out of the box marked "Old Underwear for Goodwill."

"Gee, you only have one left," Larry said.

"That's okay, we can split it. Here, I'll break it and you choose."

"We always divide up stuff like that too—that way no one can pig a bigger piece," Larry said.

"We didn't used to do that until my mom married your dad, so it must be his idea." I munched on my Ding-Dong. It was good. "Larry, are you glad they got married?"

Larry brushed some crumbs off his nose. "Yeah—I think it's pretty good. I like it now that we have our own beds over here and we don't have to sleep on the floor in sleeping bags."

"That was Mom's idea," I told him.

"It was?" he asked.

"Yeah, she told your dad that it was important for you and David to have this be like your home when you came, and so she made him buy some beds. But now they're talking about moving to a new house that has some more room, and Mom says that you and David have to help pick it out."

"Maybe we could get a farm and a horse," Larry said.

"No—Mom thinks it's dumb to live in the country—I tried to talk her into that once, but it didn't work."

"Well, I guess it won't be so bad if you move, especially if we can help pick out the house. But sometimes I get tired of everything changing so much." Larry was lying on the floor patting Martha and Laverne. They were pretty good friends now.

"Laverne's so nice," he said, scratching her ears. "How was the roller-skating party last night?"

"It was really great. I sure hope we have another one soon. When is your school going to have one?"

"Right before Thanksgiving, I think, only I'm not so sure I want to go."

"Why not?"

"Oh I dunno—maybe no one would skate with me."

"They sure would. I'll bet half the girls in your school would."

Larry smiled, then he looked over at Sara's room. She had her door open, and she and David had Shirley in there and they were dressing her up in doll clothes.

"Do you believe that? Look, Cynthia, those

jerks are dressing up that little ratty dog of theirs in doll clothes." I looked over at Sara's room and there was that stupid dog, Shirley, with a baby bonnet on her head. It looked like a rat with a baby bonnet on—it was ridiculous. I guess they heard us laughing, because they went downstairs in the kitchen and took all the doll clothes off of Shirley.

Larry and I had finished eating our Ding-Dong. "Wanna ride bikes?" I asked.

"Sure, but whose bike can I ride?"

"Oh you can ride Sara's."

We went downstairs and David and Sara were in the kitchen coloring. David always colors in the lines—he does pretty well. "That looks nice, David," I said, looking at his picture. It was a circus clown holding four balloons.

"What color should the balloons be, Cyn?" David asked. David can't say Cynthia so he always calls me Cyn.

"How 'bout yellow, red, and blue?"

"There's four," Sara said, "and I think the other one should be brown."

"Balloons aren't brown," Larry said.

"That's why you should have a brown balloon," Sara said.

I guess David thought about balloons the same way Sara did, because he made them all brown. Four brown balloons. I thought it looked awful, and Larry and I made faces to

each other when David and Sara weren't looking.

"We're going to ride bikes," I said. "Bye."

"Wait!" Sara called. "Can we come?"

"Yeah, can we come?" asked David, putting
down his crayon.

I looked at Larry. "What d'you think?" I
really wasn't that mad at them anymore. I guess
Larry wasn't either because we decided to let
them come.

We were all out riding bikes. Larry was on
Sara's bike and David was riding on the back
of it and I was riding Sara on the back of my
bike. When we were down the block from our
house, Harry Zimmerman—that creep—came
up and for no reason pushed David off Sara's
bike. I really got mad. I got off my bike and I
flattened Harry Z for zero with one punch, and
then he started yelling and saying, "Cynthia
has a boyfriend!"

Larry said, "Shut-up, she's my sister," and
he punched Harry too. Then Harry went home
to tell.

That night when I went to sleep and was
dreaming about me and Seth, I had also figured
out that Larry and David were like my real
brothers because a lot of the times I hate all
that sharing with them just like I hate all that
sharing with Sara a lot. But then other times
they're not so bad—sort of like Sara can be
okay sometimes.

Before I went to sleep I went to my closet and got my diary out of the box. I made a new page and it went like this:

THOUGHTS FOR TODAY

1. *I love Seth Rosen.*
2. *If Harry Z even touches David again, he'll really be sorry.*

ABOUT THE AUTHOR

JEAN DAVIES OKIMOTO was born in Cleveland, Ohio, and graduated with a master's degree from Antioch College. She enjoys swimming, sailing and painting, and lives in Seattle with her husband, four children and her dog LaVerne.

Also available in Archway Paperback editions is *My Mother Is Not Married to My Father*.

GROWING UP...
You Can't Run Away from It and You Don't Have To!

____ **29982 HIDING** $1.75
Norma Klein
Krii, shy and withdrawn, copes by "hiding"—until she meets Jonathan, who helps her come out of her shell. "Tremendous appeal."—West Coast Review of Books

____ **42062 FIND A STRANGER, SAY GOODBYE** $1.95
Lois Lowry
Natalie is haunted by a missing link in her life—the identity of her real mother—so she sets out on a journey to find her. "A beautifully crafted story which defines the characters with a full range of feelings and emotions."—Signal

____ **42449 THE CHEESE STANDS ALONE** $1.95
Marjorie M. Prince
Daisy takes a stand for independence as she begins to see herself in sharper focus through the eyes of the intriguing man who paints her portrait. "Absorbing." —Publishers Weekly

____ **42450 CLAUDIA, WHERE ARE YOU?** $1.95
Hila Colman
Claudia feels suffocated by her family, and runs away to New York City to find some kind of meaning in her life. "...presents a thought-provoking view of a current social problem."
—English Journal

____ **29945 LETTER PERFECT** $1.50
Charles P. Crawford
The story of three friends caught up in a blackmailing scheme. "Hard-hitting portrait of teenagers in crisis."
—Publishers Weekly

____ **41304 THE RUNAWAY'S DIARY** $1.75
Marilyn Harris
Fifteen-year-old Cat is on the road—in search of herself. "Believable and involving." —A.L.A. Booklist

____ **44238 GROWING UP IN A HURRY** $1.95
Winifred Madison
Karen discovers she is pregnant and must make a painful decision. "A hard-hitting and brilliantly written novel."
—Publishers Weekly

If your bookseller does not have the titles you want, you may order them by sending the retail price (plus 50¢ postage and handling for each order—New York State and New York City residents please add appropriate sales tax) to POCKET BOOKS, Dept. AGU, 1230 Avenue of the Americas, New York, N.Y. 10020. Send check or money order—no cash or C.O.Ds—and be sure to include your name and address. Allow up to six weeks for delivery.   198

ARCHWAY PAPERBACKS from Pocket Books

YOUNG LOVE,
FIRST LOVE
Stories of Romance

____ **44386 SEVENTEENTH SUMMER** $2.50
Maureen Daly
*When Angie meets Jack she is drawn into a golden summer of
first love. "Simply, eloquently, Maureen Daly tells one how
youth in love really feels."*—The New York Times

____ **41327 GIFT OF GOLD** $1.95
Beverly Butler
*Cathy, blind since the age of fourteen, needs courage to pursue
her career as a speech therapist—and to make up her mind
about the two very different men in her life. "Unusual and
inspiring novel...a tender love story."*—Publishers Weekly

____ **42456 MORNING IS A LONG TIME COMING** $1.95
Bette Greene
The author of Summer of My German Soldier *continues the
bittersweet saga of Patty Bergen. "Compelling first-person
narrative about love and human relationships."*
—*A.L.A. Booklist (starred review)

____ **29916 THE TESTING OF CHARLIE HAMMELMAN** $1.75
Jerome Brooks
*Charlie faces a crisis and feels he can't talk to anybody—then
he meets Shirley and finds love and understanding.
"A convincing, upbeat and contemporary story."*
—*A.L.A. Booklist (starred review)

____ **44232 THE DISTANT SUMMER** $1.95
Sarah Patterson
*"For romance, adventure and plain good reading, curl up with
The Distant Summer."*—Seventeen *"A beautiful, romantic
story, one that stays with you long after you've read the book.
I loved it."*—Judy Blume

If your bookseller does not have the titles you want, you may order them by sending the retail price (plus
50¢ postage and handling for each order—New York State and New York City residents please add appropriate sales tax) to: POCKET BOOKS, Dept. AYA, 1230 Avenue of the Americas, New York, N.Y. 10020. Send
check or money order—no cash or C.O.D.s—and be sure to include your name and address. Allow up to six
weeks for delivery.

244

ARCHWAY PAPERBACKS from Pocket Books

ELLEN CONFORD KNOWS...

the world we live in...
and the struggles to grow up in it!

_____**ME AND THE TERRIBLE TWO**   (41769/$1.75)
Dorrie knows one thing worse than having your best friend next door move out; having two creepy boys move in. "Good fun..."—A.L.A. Booklist

_____**FELICIA THE CRITIC**   (43924/$1.95)
When Felicia gives her opinion, everyone gets mad. But when she doesn't, they get madder. "Fresh, entertaining..."—Horn Book

_____**THE ALFRED G. GRAEBNER MEMORIAL HIGH SCHOOL HANDBOOK OF RULES AND REGULATIONS: A NOVEL** (41673/$1.95)
The hazards of high school that Julie's handbook never warned her about. "...a funny first-person narrative full of typical teenage dilemmas..."—A.L.A. Booklist

_____**AND THIS IS LAURA**   (44234/$1.95)
Is Laura's talent for seeing into the future a gift or a curse? "Conford is at her best in this funny novel."—Publishers Weekly

_____**HAIL, HAIL CAMP TIMBERWOOD**   (42685/$1.95)
Melanie falls in love for the first time. "...an appealing, lighthearted story."—A.L.A. Booklist

_____**THE LUCK OF POKEY BLOOM**   (44233/$1.95)
If Pokey enters enough contests, she's bound to get lucky sometime. "...well-crafted, fast-paced, and freshly imagined..."—Horn Book

If your bookseller does not have the titles you want, you may order them by sending the retail price (plus 50¢ postage and handling for each order—New York State and New York City residents please add appropriate sales tax) to POCKET BOOKS Dept. AEC, 1230 Avenue of the Americas, New York, N.Y. 10020. Send check or money order—no cash or C.O.D.s—and be sure to include your name and address. Allow six weeks for delivery.

ARCHWAY PAPERBACKS from Pocket Books   245